AMBER PALMER

THE NIGHT RUNS RED

THE WICKED DARK DUOLOGY

BOOK ONE

Complete Editing Services performed by Heather Nix

Alpha/Beta: Liz Mayer and Sarah Maricle

Cover Typography: Amanda at Eternal Geekery

Cover Art: Elizianna.The.One

When Calia Darrow, a descendant of fae royalty, learns she is to be wed to prominent vampyre Rion D'arcy, she accepts her fate—not that she has a choice. With an age-old curse binding their families together in an attempt to balance power, Calia and Rion must marry unless they wish to forfeit their lives.

After a tumultuous ceremony, Calia finds herself isolated in a sprawling gothic mansion with a husband who wants nothing to do with her. When a foiled abduction attempt leaves her vulnerable, Calia sees a glimmer of hope that perhaps there is more to Rion than she thought.

As the blood moon approaches, Calia must face an unknown enemy with only the assistance of the mysterious Rion D'Arcy. Will the truth come to light, or will the night run red with Calia's blood?

For every single person searching for strength, and for those who are finding theirs for the first time.

Also for my Papa, who instilled my obsession for everything paranormal and fantastical. I wish you were here to see what I've done with that passion.

playlist

*Music is essential to my writing, and so I've compiled a
pretty badass playlist on Spotify!*

content warnings

<u>**This book is intended for those 18+.**</u>

- Graphic Sexual Content
- Minor Blood/Bite Play
- Kidnapping
- Attempted SA
- Body Dismemberment
- Depictions of Gore/Blood
- Depictions of Torture
- *Very* Adult Language
- Insecure Thoughts by FMC
- Arranged Marriage
- Mentions of Dermatillomania
- Suicide

Long ago, when the world was little more than rubble and ash, one family reigned over all living beings. First King of the Fae, Calix Darrow, was a benevolent ruler, ensuring peace within his kingdom. The fae, witches, vampyres, and mortals united to form the High City of Kallistos—a unique utopia for all who dwelled within its walls, as well as the permanent home of the royal family.

Fae magic was initially bound by the laws of nature, coursing through the land as earth, wind, water, and fire. But as the centuries passed, their powers evolved. Unions between the fae and the witches caused offspring to be of both worlds—the divine and the elemental—thus ushering in a new era of magic.

Somewhere along the way, peace began to falter as evil crept through the land, poisoning the minds of its Inhabitants. Vampyres became infatuated with amplifying their gifts, craving more magic than they were blessed with. They became relentless as they grappled for power that was not theirs to hold. Arowan D'Arcy rose above the rest, calling those who shared his beliefs to action. Soon, what was once a prosperous land was reduced to cinders as fae and vampyre turned on one another, shattering the hard won peace and creating a war unlike anything seen before.

As the death toll rose across Auria, King Calix desperately searched for a way to quell the uprising and bring peace again to the land. Mortals were slaughtered, witches hunted for their magic—forced to surrender it or risk their lives. Covens dispersed and fled, fearing for their lives and the lives of those they loved. They pleaded with the king to end the madness, but he saw no way out. Not until the night before the fabled blood moon did his answer come to him in a dream.

The following day his vision became apparent, and the king set out to find his salvation. Standing amongst a field of poppies, a woman knelt and prayed beneath the red sky. Golden marks along her skin shone under the moon's light, her hair the color of freshly fallen winter snow. She turned, fixing her bright, luminous eyes on him before speaking in a language he hadn't heard in centuries.

"What is it that you seek?" she asked him, her voice soft and tender. The woman listened as he divulged his fears regarding the war Arowan waged on his people and land. As he finished, she looked back up to the

moon before closing her eyes. "There shall be consequences—"

But the king interrupted her, insisting she do what
she could to save the land. Her hands lifted to the sky as
she chanted once again.

The wind howled around them as lightning tore
through the night. In the distance, thunder sounded
from the heavens above like the pounding of war drums.
He fell to his knees at the sight, both wonder and fear
filling his thoughts. The air was permeated with the
scent of copper and iron. Soon, the king's hands were
covered in droplets of blood that fell from the sky.

The woman dropped her hands, pressing her face to
the wet, crimson ground below as she finished her
prayers. She turned to the king, who'd fallen back in
awe of the power he'd just witnessed. "It is done," she
whispered. Her voice had grown hoarse, barely audible
over her heavy breathing. "When the sun rises, the
vampyres will be forced into a world of darkness. They
shall never feel the warmth of sun upon their skin.
Those who try will forfeit their lives." The king thanked
her, crying joyfully at this good news, but the woman
was not done. "Beware, King, for nature demands a
balance."

"What have you done?" he cursed, a quiet rage
bleeding into his short-lived happiness.

She turned on him, using her magic to wrap death-
touched fingers around his throat. "I tried to warn you
that this magic would have consequences, but you
refused to hear them. Now, you shall listen and take

heed; this agreement begins with your heir. While the vampyres will never know warmth, your people shall never look upon the stars. From now until the end of time, when the blood moon rises in the sky every one hundred years, nature will demand the joining of Darrow and D'Arcy. Those chosen will be marked by the fates. Should either refuse, by the time the cycle has ended, both lives will be taken as payment. The key to both your salvation and damnation relies on a fragile balance of power between your descendents and those of your Vampyre foe."

The king wanted to ask more, beg her for clarification, but as the woman released her hold on his throat, her form dissipated, blowing away in the wind. He was left on his knees, watching the sun rise on his broken kingdom.

Word spread quickly from town to town as the fae guards rode hard to disperse the news before nightfall. As neither creature could walk under the same sky, their bloodshed came to a halt. Arowan wrote to the king, demanding an audience. They met in the tunnels beneath the palace with only their children at their backs. He ordered the king to reverse the effects of the curse, however there was nothing to be done. Their children had already been marked.

The king explained how the witch had told him that their children would be forced to wed as punishment for their bloodshed. Arowan took his son and left, laughing at the king's gullibility and pleas for his daughter's life.

Within a fortnight, as the moon returned to its

natural glow, both men were forced to come to terms with their curse as they watched their children's ashes scatter on the wind.

As the centuries passed, animosity grew between the two families as they watched their children be forced into a union with their enemies. Despite the years and their long lives, neither vampyre nor fae had found a way to end the cycle and free their kind from the new laws set forth by their creators.

As Kallistos was ushered into a new, modern age, the monarchy crumbled. As a concession, each faction elected members to represent their interest on a new council. War was no longer fought on battlefields but behind closed doors where corruption ran deep and hungry hands grabbed for control that was never theirs to hold. Time did nothing to mend old wounds, and the history of the past slipped further from the minds of the present.

one

A bolt of lightning snaked across the darkened sky, illuminating my room and the body draped across mine. The storm had been raging for days, remaining just as angry and violent as it was when it began. I'd held onto hope that it would postpone the events of the next few hours, though the thought was quickly shut down by my father this morning during breakfast.

No, I would be forced to walk down the aisle tomorrow and sign my life away to a man I've never met to appease a vendetta I played no part in.

When I was a little girl, I dreamed of my wedding day. There would be flowers as far as the eye could see, filling the room with their sweet, aromatic scents and the most delectable food money could buy. I would wear a dress made just for me, one crafted with hand-spun lace that shimmered as soon as the light touched it. My father would walk me down the aisle before passing me off to the person I loved. He would kiss my cheek and tell me how much he loved me and how I'd made him proud before turning away to stand by my mother. They would cry, of course, because I was their only daughter.

But as I grew up, I realized that life was no fairytale. A happily ever after was never promised, nor would it come.

My impending marriage was an olive branch to keep the peace amongst two warring factions. And because I was born with a mark on my back that designated me as nature's chosen, my life has been tied to someone else's.

The specifics of our contract were handled behind closed doors, where the men smoked cigars and drank fine whiskey while making decisions that affected my life. It didn't matter if I wanted to do it or not.

If I refused, I would die.

As I stared out the window, I resented the city below. It glistened under the night sky, coming alive under the thrum and power of the full moon. Even I could feel the call of the inky blanket of stars beckoning me to stand beneath their glow.

I'd never seen the stars without the barrier of enchanted glass, but I'd always felt a calling to them. I longed to dance beneath their subtle glow, to be kissed by the night's cold wind. But I was cursed, as all fae were, to never know what the night felt like.

This was the closest I would ever get, and that was only thanks to the magic my family's money could buy. The local covens stayed far away from business relating to the fae and the vampyres, but even they could not refuse the allure of lucrative endeavors.

When I was five, I'd become obsessed with the darkness and what lingered in it. My mother had the power of illusion and would cast stars upon my ceiling every night when the thick, steel shades descended across every window in the house. As I grew up, though, I could tell it wasn't real. The call to the true darkness never abated, no matter how hard she tried to pacify my curiosity.

Against my father's will, she approached the witches and begged for a solution—a way for her daughter, who so loved the dark, to appease the curiosity of her mind and body. At first, they denied her request, but it didn't deter her. She came back every week, leaving offerings at their doorstep, until the covens finally agreed. They warned, however, that what they did for one, they would have to do for the other.

Within the year that followed, the homes of the two factions were fitted with enchanted glass that allowed fae to bask in the night and vampyres to walk in the sun. When my father found out what she'd done, he'd taken out his fury on her body.

"Are you still awake, Calia?" Elom asked, his voice raspy from sleep. He snaked an arm around my waist, adjusting his grip and pulling me close.

I softly hummed, watching the rain assault the glass as Elom's fingers traced soft circles along my ribs. I hated when he did that, hated the sensation of anyone touching my stomach and sides. I pushed his hand away, feeling him flinch from my indifference.

"We could run away together," he said, leaning forward and kissing my shoulder. "I'm not wealthy, and I couldn't offer you the comfort you're used to, but I do well enough. I've got enough money to last us a while. We could get settled somewhere else, maybe across the sea. I've heard the countryside is amazing; you've mentioned it before. We could figure out the rest once we get there."

He rambled on and on, not stopping until he nearly ran out of breath. It was a sweet notion, but the thought made me just as nauseous as the future awaiting me tomorrow. Elom was kind—the type who saw the good in everyone and everything, no matter the situation. It was what drew me to him when I'd first laid eyes on him at the coffee shop I frequented on the way to my cousin's house. It reminded me of the kindness people said they saw in my mother. I believed it was fate or whatever divine intervention the old gods prophesized.

It didn't take long for that kindness to sour like curdled milk in my stomach. Perhaps I was more like my father than I cared to admit. Nevertheless, Elom soothed the loneliness and kept my cold heart from freezing over completely. It was selfish to keep him on, especially when I learned of the depth of his feelings. He'd cried for thirty minutes when I told him of the betrothal and how quickly the ceremony would take place. I almost felt pity for him, though it quickly changed to indifference the longer we sat together. To live a life with him would be a death sentence, and I had no plans of dying just yet.

"As sweet as the thought is, it isn't an option," I said with a sigh. "And you deserve to love someone who can give you a fulfilled life. That'll never be the case with me."

We'd fought about this on more than one occasion. I was the foolish one who kept this situation-ship going purely for selfish reasons. Regardless of his clingy nature, Elom was a good lover. He always aimed to please me first, multiple times, in fact, before he sought his pleasure. Since I was destined for a life of self-enjoyment, I wanted to be selfish a bit longer.

Beyond that, my duty and title as a Darrow would not permit me to marry who I chose. I was marked from birth to be used as a sacrifice to an eternal curse. My family descended from the true line of fae royalty who ruled long before the council took their place. Both my father and my aunt were members, an ode to the old ways.

This was the way my life was always destined to be. Even without the curse, Elom would never have made it onto the list of suitors. Even though he was fae, he had no title or money to offer, no meaningful connections to be bartered to my father for my hand.

Elom's fingers halted on my thigh, and he looked up at me, his shadowy eyes nearly blending into the darkness lingering throughout my bedroom. "To hell with your father. Shouldn't you have a say in your own life and future?"

I pinched the bridge of my nose, attempting to soothe the headache that was beginning to blossom there. "It's not that simple."

The death clause in the permanent marriage contract between the Darrows and the D'Arcys was kept secret, and I could not reveal the knowledge to anyone outside of our bloodline. The two chosen to wed were marked at birth, born into a world where their destiny had already been decided by fate.

Elom sat up, exposing my naked body to the chill air. A rebuttal sat on his lips, ready to fire away, but then his eyes dipped lower and lower until he stared at the soft center between my thighs. It was his mistake, one he hadn't intended to make, but all thoughts seemed to eddy from his mind as he took in my body.

His gaze would have bothered me before, but now I welcomed and embraced it. I tried to be proud of how I looked, but I'd have been a fool not to notice the haughty looks from others as I walked by. Even as a child, I was teased and tormented about my body. I was never thin, and while I tried to tell myself I would grow out of it, I never did. Instead, my figure grew fuller. I embraced my curves—celebrated them, even—so long as people never touched me unless I invited them to.

It'd taken a long time to get to this point, and I still had moments of weakness when I looked in the mirror. Those days had me crawling into bed, wearing oversized clothing to hide myself, and crying into my pillow. I looked nothing like the women in my family, only inheriting their tall height. But where they were willowy, possessing a perceived perfection I'd never never been graced with, I was blessed with curves and thick thighs. My stomach was supple, sporting lines of stretch marks along my permanent pooch.

I ran a hand up my body, softly caressing my skin with the tips of my nails. Elom inhaled deeply, noting the change in my scent that told him I wanted this as badly as he did. Men didn't take long to become distracted, and Elom was no exception. Though I could tell he wanted to argue, to fight for me and hope I fought for him in return, he said no more as he leaned in and kissed me deeply.

The hours I had remaining passed in a blur—Elom kept me up with his skilled fingers and tongue until the sun rose over the peaks of the mountains in the distance. He looked in my direction wistfully as he slipped out of my door. His brown eyes were full of regret for everything he didn't say. "I hope you find some semblance of happiness within this, Calia. But if you don't, then my offer still stands."

I nodded, offering him all I could—a simple smile. Because it didn't matter if I found happiness or not. That wasn't the point of this. And even if it was, my happiness didn't lie with him. He took my silence as dismissal and slipped through the door and out of my life for good.

two

T he silence was the first thing I noticed as I opened my eyes. Sun streamed in from the windows, illuminating my bedroom in a soft glow. The rain had stopped, and the storm passed. It seemed like a perfect day.

Fuck.

I pushed up onto my elbows, blinking at the bright light. I glanced over at the clock sitting on my night-stand. It was only seven, but I knew it was only a matter of time before someone came knocking on my door and bursting inside.

A small picture sat next to the clock, one I tried to look at every morning as a reminder to seize the day. In it, my mom's arms were draped around me, holding me close. A traveling carnival had come to town, and I'd begged my parents to take me. My father said no, telling me it was unbecoming to be seen at something so mundane, but my mom understood. She'd excused me from school the following day, and we spent hours getting lost in greasy food, games that were clearly rigged, and rides that were most likely unsafe. We'd laughed until we were hoarse and asked a random passerby to take our picture in front of the cotton candy machine.

It was one of my last memories of her before her death, and it was still one of the happiest days of my life.

"I'll make you proud, Mom," I said, kissing my fingers and touching the glass on the frame. I always waited a moment, hoping she would respond or give me some sign from beyond, but I sat in silence as always.

I stumbled out of bed, peeling out of my clothes and turning on the shower. Frigid water came streaming out from the faucet, hitting my arm before I could pull it back. "Shit," I mumbled, wiping my hand on the towel hanging on the wall. I sighed, looking around the room before ambling over to the small speaker perched on the shelf nearby and turning it on, fumbling for a playlist on my phone to brighten my mood. I settled on one, listening to the soft rock tones fill the space before rechecking the water temperature.

As I slipped inside, the heat from the water soon steamed up the glass around me, encasing me in my private bubble. There were no pressures or social expectations, and certainly no betrothals. There was only me in this singular, perfect moment in time. Without the weight of the day, I felt like I could breathe. I lathered my hair with shampoo and conditioner, enjoying the soft mint scent tingling my nose.

I heard my bedroom door creak open, footsteps quickly following. "Calia?"

"In here!" I called over the music, enjoying my last moments of peace before the day began. I finished my shower quickly, rinsing the remaining products out of my hair before turning the water off and stepping out of the shower.

"I don't know how you can hear yourself think with your music so loud," my cousin, Brielle, mused. "Hell, I could hear it down the hall."

I smirked. "And on a scale of one to ten, how pissed is my father?"

She tapped her chin. "Hm, I think he's simmering around a seven right now, but I don't know if you caused that. Or at least, not entirely."

I shrugged my shoulders, staring at myself in the mirror as I toweled my hair. "I can never tell with him. You'd think he'd be more excited to get me out of the house and marry me off. Especially since he can't stand looking at me most days."

Brielle wrapped her arm around my shoulder, leaning her cheek on my head. "I wish we could have gotten you out of this mess, Cal. You know, my mom tried everything she could—"

I waved her off, stepping out of her embrace and turning away. She'd done more than enough for me in the years since my mom died. She'd stepped in without hesitation and involved me in everything she did with

Brielle. I wondered if my cousin hated sharing her mom with me, but she never said anything.

The one time I'd brought it up, I was seventeen and drunk off my ass on a bottle of wine she'd snuck out of her mom's liquor cabinet. We'd gone up to the roof, staring at the stars as we passed the bottle back and forth until I got the courage to ask. She'd sat up so fast that she nearly fell off the roof and told me if I ever asked her something that stupid again, she'd kick my ass.

We never brought it up again.

Brielle sighed, running a hand through her hair. "Alright, alright," she said, throwing her hands up. "I won't push, but I hope you know we're here for you, Cal. Just because you're marrying into the D'Arcy family doesn't mean you don't still belong to us. You're still our princess, and you're my cousin. My sister." The last word hung in the air as she quickly wiped away a fallen tear.

I turned to face her, taking in her blue eyes that had become rimmed with silver. She was much older than me, but you couldn't tell, given her fae heritage. Brielle was over two hundred and still just as beautiful and full of youth as any other twenty-something you'd see on the street. Her blonde hair had always been long, falling down her back in soft curls. It was the type that made you jealous, trying everything to replicate it when you knew some things could only be obtained by near-perfect genetics.

"Bri, c'mon," I said, walking toward her and grabbing

her hands. "You act like I'm going to attend my funeral. Nothing will change between us."

Her eyes grew wide, turning her best pout on full force. "But what if they don't let you see us?"

I laughed. "It's not like I'm going to prison, either. Listen, they'll deal with it. There's nothing they can do to keep us apart. Besides, this whole agreement is supposed to unify our peoples, not further the divide."

She worried her bottom lip. "This just feels wrong. I don't know, I can't explain it. I feel like I'm never going to see you again."

"Never gonna happen, Bri."

She laughed, though the sound seemed half-hearted. "I don't know how you can be so calm. You're about to walk into the viper's den. *Literally.*"

I wanted to tell her I was the opposite of calm and that I was so terrified I'd barely eaten or slept in three days. Or that the heavy weight in the pit of my stomach seemed to grow with each hour that passed. But I couldn't tell her any of that because if I did, she would run straight to my aunt.

So instead, I put on my best attempt at a smile and shrugged. "Because I know it'll be fine. Plus, Rion D'Arcy is next-level hot. There isn't a woman in Kallistos who hasn't thought about fucking him, and now I get to marry him. It's a win-win."

"I know what you're doing, you know," she said, tapping her long nails against my doorframe. "You're not near as clever as you think."

"I have absolutely no idea what you're talking

about." I moved past her, walking into my closet and searching for the outfit that had arrived yesterday from the D'Arcy family. The gift had been packaged in an ornate box stamped with their family crest. It was obnoxiously done, a 'fuck-you' to my father that his only daughter would no longer belong to him.

Brielle whistled lowly. "At least they have good taste," she mused, lifting the silk bridal set from the box where I'd left it.

"Thank the gods for small mercies, huh?" I said, walking over and changing quickly. The outfit comprised three pieces—an ivory embroidered lingerie set, a silk button-down shirt with matching shorts, and a floor-length robe.

There was a small notecard on top of the clothing that I tossed back in the box. Brielle, ever the nosey one, picked it up. "Welcome to the family," she skimmed it, glancing at me over the edge. "He didn't even sign his name—if he wrote this. The handwriting is better than my mom's."

"I hadn't noticed," I said, pulling my hair out of my face. Though wearing clothing that cost more than a vehicle, I felt plain as I looked at my reflection in the mirror. My skin was pale, with no sign of the soft smattering of freckles I loved. I'd gotten them from my mom, and their absence only made me miss her more. I'd spent more time inside since my father informed me of my impending nuptials, holing myself up in my room and blaring music to drown out the noise in my head. There were dark circles under my eyes—no surprise there—and their presence muted my green eyes.

Brielle came up behind me, wrapping her arms around my neck as she stared at me through the mirror. "You don't look like a blushing bride on her wedding day, Cal. You look like you're getting ready for a funeral. Well, minus the banging ensemble."

I sighed, bringing my hand up to clasp her own. "That's because I'm not. This is a business deal. Nothing more, nothing less. And it will get me out of my father's house and away from his rage. That's what we've been trying to do for years, and now it's finally happening, even if it's not how we wanted."

There was a knock on the door, and Brielle stepped away to answer it. Kai, one of my father's many security guards, stuck his head through before she had a chance. "Your car's here, Miss Darrow. They'll escort you and Miss Thorne to the venue." He blushed as he looked at Brielle, who only batted her doe eyes at him.

"Can you tell them I'll be down in five minutes?" I asked, knots beginning to form in my stomach. I couldn't let it show, though. My father could sense fear like a shark could scent blood, and his wrath was the last thing I wanted to endure today.

Kai left with a dip of his head, closing the door behind him. "He is *so* hot," Brielle whined.

"Don't you already have a boyfriend?" I teased, knowing that she didn't do relationships at all.

Brielle leveled me with a stare. "I have a friend I see occasionally for sex, Cal. That is far from the same thing." She paused, noticing my furrowed brows. "Hey, are you okay? What can I do?"

I looked around the room one last time, savoring the bitter taste of freedom. There were so many memories here, and while I couldn't give a shit about most of them, I knew I'd miss how I felt closer to my mom when I was here.

I gave her a half-hearted smile. "Nothing, nothing," I said, waving a hand. "I guess it's just hitting me that I'm not coming back here."

"At all?" Brielle asked, looking around, and I shook my head. "You haven't packed anything! Who is moving your stuff?"

That was the clause I'd fought with my father over the most. My soon-to-be husband said I couldn't bring anything when I left. Everything would be furnished for me, something about ensuring I matched the image the family maintained. While I didn't mind the thought of getting a new wardrobe, I'd asked my father if my betrothed would 'allow' me to bring the picture of my mom. I couldn't bear leaving it behind to be thrown in the trash when my father undoubtedly turned my room into something ostentatious like a sauna.

My father had only said one thing: "*No.*"

That was that—even if it broke my fucking heart.

When I told Brielle as much, she looked horrified. She marched over to the frame, grabbed it, and stuffed it in her purse. "We'll smuggle the damn thing in if we have to," she whispered conspiratorially.

"Miss Darrow? We need to leave now if we are going

to keep to the schedule," Kai said, peeking his head back in and lowering his voice. "And your father has already threatened to dismiss me if I go back downstairs without you." He cringed as my father yelled something intelligible from below us.

Brielle squeezed my hand, making sure I knew she would be by my side no matter what. "Ready to get married?"

"You look *beautiful*," Brielle chimed as the stylist stepped away from where I sat. We'd been plucked, prodded, and primped within an inch of our lives since we stepped through the door. The bridal suite was littered with every dainty finger food we could imagine, and servers kept the mimosas flowing. My stomach was too tied up in knots to eat, but that didn't stop me from reaching for my glass every time they filled it.

The cathedral was breathtaking, but I knew it was chosen for one reason only. It had been blessed by the witches of old to be an eternal meeting place for the warring factions. Beneath our feet were the bones of those that had come before us, and they blessed the space to be exempt from the curse for the duration of the blood moon. It was their way of ensuring our union was always possible.

My long, dark auburn hair fell down my back in soft

waves, the front tendrils loosely tied back and braided with pale flowers intertwined. My makeup artist, who was finishing up on Bri, had given me two options when we'd arrived. Both were nearly identical, so I didn't know why my choice mattered, but I selected the one that came with dark red lipstick instead of the one an infinitesimal shade lighter.

My dress hung in one of the stained-glass windows, the colors dancing along the wall as the sun shone through the panes. My father spent a ridiculous amount of money to fly in a designer, something he grumbled over even though I'd told him it wasn't necessary. However, he refused to be outdone by my future in-laws, who'd footed most of the bill for the wedding.

The gown was designed to fit my body like a glove, showing off my curves in a way that had me thanking the gods for their existence. Why couldn't I look like this every day? The sleeves were long and sheer, save for the vines of lace that flowed down my arms from the bottom of the dress. It was perfect, both elegant and sexy. Enough to hopefully entice the most desirable man in the city, who had no choice but to accept me as his bride.

I didn't know much about Rion D'Arcy—only that he was talked about in every tabloid we had, and every word was scandalous. Each week there was a new woman, or two, draped on his arm as he smiled for the camera. Still, the man was a mystery despite his very public life. I'd hardly heard him utter more than two sentences unless he was speaking in front of a crowd on behalf of his family.

That thought loomed overhead like an inky cloud, diminishing any hope or excitement I could have. Even if I'd been given a choice, it wouldn't change the outcome. In the time since the last union, tensions between the fae and the vampyres had begun to rage out of control; innocent lives were lost, caught in the cross-fire as collateral damage.

A knock interrupted my musing, Brielle and I glancing anxiously at the door. The event coordinator had popped her head in earlier to tell me that my betrothed and his family wanted to meet before the ceremony, and judging by the number of voices I heard on the other side, I knew this was it.

"You can do this," Brielle murmured as she reached for my hand. "And I'll be right by your side if you need me."

No sooner had I dipped my head in thanks when a tall, slender woman waltzed through the door. I recognized her quickly from the numerous tabloids and newspaper articles I'd seen her face plastered across. Leonora D'Arcy's perfect silky blonde hair was swept back into a low chignon, drawing attention to her delicate frame. She sat down on the large sofa opposite us and was quickly followed by a beautiful, tall man whose dazzling smile nearly knocked the breath out of my lungs. Between his burnished gold eyes and the slightest hint of dimples, I was speechless.

Too bad he isn't my fiancé.

As if summoned, the man in question walked through the door with a huff of exasperation, fixing his blazing gaze on me.

three

Rion D'Arcy's black hair was held just out of his eyes, perfecting that stylishly sexy, ruffled look that every man dreamed of achieving. Stormy, peppered eyes swept over me, causing my insecurities to rise and strike my carefully curated confidence. I fought the urge to shrink in on myself, knowing a man like him would never respect me if I showed weakness. His mother's barely contained sneer told me all I needed to know.

He pulled at the sleeves of his black tuxedo, impeccably tailored to show off his perfect physique. Around the cuffs at his wrist, faint markings of tattoos peeked out. I couldn't deny the attraction I felt toward him. Fuck me, every part of him oozed sex appeal, and given the infinitesimal smirk he sent my way, he damn well knew it.

But that attraction was only surface level. Once someone saw past the persona he portrayed—the disgustingly wealthy bachelor who had no cares except for getting his dick wet—they'd notice the red-soaked hands from the lives he'd taken.

The room remained painfully silent as he sat beside his mother, who was already glaring daggers in my direction. Brielle and I exchanged glances at one another. She raised an eyebrow at me, nodding in their direction slyly as if to say, *"Break the silence, you idiot!"*

I cleared my throat, not knowing what I should say. Neither of them looked pleased with what they saw, which was chipping away at the shaky confidence I'd attempted to piece together all morning. But if I'd learned anything over my twenty-nine years, it was how to fake what I didn't feel.

"It's wonderful to meet you all. I understand our situation is delicate, but rest assured I will do whatever I can to ease tensions between our people," I said, attempting to keep my voice even.

Rion and his mother remained silent, and I fought against the embarrassment rising in my chest as his mother rolled her eyes. *Have I severely misread the situation?* As I looked away, the suave fair-haired stranger on the end gave me a confident smile that eased my nerves a fraction.

Keep calm, Calia. Don't let them get under your skin.

"*Yes*," Rion's mother said slowly. "Wonderful indeed. As you know, my name is Leonora D'Arcy." Condescension dripped from her words, telling me she didn't find this wonderful at all. Her deep crimson gown was littered with dark gemstones, while elbow-length black gloves seemed painted to her skin and matched the obsidian-colored necklace draped against her chest.

Before the silence could linger, Brielle gave a small wave. "Hi, I'm Brielle. Calia's cousin." Her eyes lingered on the mystery man. "I'm not quite sure we're familiar with *you.*"

"That means I'm doing my job right," he said with a grin before standing up and approaching us. He stuck his hand out in greeting. "Jasper Sinclaire. Mr. D'Arcy's bodyguard." His burnished eyes met mine, causing a warm sensation to fill my stomach. He was beautiful and charming—a wild comfort in this utter shitstorm of a day. "We'll see a lot of each other in the months to come until we sort out your security."

"My security?" I asked, the words breaking the trance I'd been in. I'd never had my own security in my life. The only exception was the week after my mother's death, when Aunt Vivian insisted on it. Once my father emerged from his bedroom with bloodshot eyes, though, he'd dismissed them without a second thought and slapped me across the face after they stepped out the door. I was no match for my father's unparalleled fae strength, especially not at such a young age. I'd nursed a black eye for three days until it faded enough to return to school without raising suspicion.

"Yes," Jasper said, looking uncomfortable suddenly. He drew his hand back, and I glanced around his frame, seeing Rion's clenched fist. "With yours and Mr. D'Arcy's union, there are likely to be people who will not be as welcoming as others. But you do not need to worry about that. It is my job to mitigate any issues that may arise."

I leaned back in my chair, crossing my legs at my ankles. "I see. Well, I appreciate you taking the time to introduce yourself." It wasn't lost on me that Rion hadn't made any effort. Which was fine. I didn't mind. At least, that's what I tried to tell myself.

Without warning, Rion quickly rose to his feet and fastened the button on his jacket before holding out a hand for his mother to take. "I shall see you soon," he said softly, averting his gaze. I hadn't had a chance to respond before they left our room as quickly as they came in. Jasper, to his credit, nodded and smiled politely before stepping out of the door.

Brielle and I stared at one another in shock. "Did that just happen?" I asked, turning back toward the door. "He didn't even say hello."

Her brows furrowed as she leaned back and fiddled with the charm bracelet around her wrist. Her mom had gotten us matching ones when I turned eighteen, and they were something we always wore. Something was on her mind—she only quieted like that when she was holding something back, but after a few moments of terse silence, I decided not to push.

I rolled my shoulders, releasing the pent-up tension clinging to my body. I quickly settled back into my chair and picked up another mimosa before thinking about the silver-eyed devil who'd already turned my world upside down.

"Oh, my girl…" I turned around at my aunt's strangled whisper as she entered the bridal suite door. My uncle followed up behind her, resting his hand on her shoulder.

Brielle helped me into my dress, latching the last clasp between my shoulder blades. Their watery gaze met mine through the mirror, and I fought to keep the tears at bay. Her smile was weak, but her eyes softened as she approached and scanned me from head to toe.

As she drew near, Brielle stepped away, and my aunt wrapped her arms around my middle. I rested my hand on hers. "Thank you for coming, Aunt Viv. I couldn't do this without you." The only response she gave was a tighter hug.

My aunt and uncle had always been my haven, treating me no differently than they had Brielle or her brother Xavier. I'd known more love than I ever hoped to have between them. Vivian never backed down from my father, regardless of the venom he spewed her way. When he banned her from seeing me, she simply found a way to sneak me out by placing guards on her payroll, rather than my father's.

The thought of going extended periods without seeing them had my mimosas threatening to reappear. But surely, if this was for peace, they wouldn't ostracize me from my family. It seemed counterproductive, but what did I know about arranged marriages and peace treaties?

As Vivian loosened her grip, Castor closed the door and pulled her into his side. Their relationship was one I'd always hoped to have. He'd forsaken everything to be with her, and their love had stood the test of time. There were so many instances I'd caught him staring at her when she wasn't paying attention, and each time, I watched him fall more in love with her than he had been a second before.

"Are you okay with this, little star?" my uncle asked, glancing down at his wife.

There was a knock on the door. Jasper poked his head through the door, mouth gaping as he saw me. He covered it up with a quick, unconvincing cough. "My apologies. I didn't mean to interrupt, but it's time."

I'd never been more thankful for an interruption because it stopped me from having to answer my uncle's question. Brielle was the only one who knew I'd thought about saying no. Judging by the narrow-eyed glare she was giving me, I'd bet she wasn't happy about the lie either.

All we needed to do was get through the day.

four

We filed out of the bridal room quietly after Jasper had interrupted us. I was a mess of nerves and nausea, my stomach turning over at the thought of leaving everything I knew behind. My hands shook as I reached down and gripped the skirts of my wedding dress to keep myself from tripping. How I was supposed to make it down the aisle without falling face-first was still a mystery.

I loved how my aunt and uncle cared for me, but that same love weighed harder on my conscience than I anticipated. Their burning stares bore into my back, only adding to the suffocating silence surrounding us. Each footstep was a death knell, perfectly in time with my thundering heart.

The uncomfortable tension only grew as we stepped into the grand foyer. My father stood beneath the tall ceilings near the middle of the room with his hands clasped behind him. His dark brown hair was combed back, allowing the sharp-tipped ears of our kind to be on full display. A deep scowl already marred his features, his nose screwing up in disgust as he studied the man at my side.

"Finally," he said gruffly, his pale eyes looking me over. His scrutiny was palpable, and I felt every bit of it claw its way beneath my skin. "I suppose you look tolerable."

I was used to his insults. I had heard them for much of my life—but each barbed insult still felt like a whip across my skin that left me raw and bleeding. Castor let out a low growl behind me, but my father didn't acknowledge him. They had a strained relationship at best, and it was better for everyone involved to keep their interactions limited, seeing as they typically ended with traded blows and bloodied fists.

I couldn't handle it if that happened today.

"Thank you, Father," I said, dipping my head. "And I appreciate you gracing us with your presence." It was a lie, but his ego wouldn't let him see it for what it was. Instead, he would use my words to fill himself with false bravado.

"As if I had a choice," he scoffed.

I lowered my gaze, ready for him to launch into a tirade regarding keeping our family line pure. He always said his greatest curse was falling in love with my mother and being damned with me for a daughter.

I was a disappointment to him in every way. At least

that's what he told me every time he'd had too much bourbon.

Before the familiar urge to apologize could creep across my tongue, Jasper angled his body in front of me. His massive frame dwarfed my father, who, while tall, could not compare to the vampyre's muscular frame. Once upon a time, when the fae ruled over the world and fought their wars with steel and magic, perhaps he would have measured up. But those days were long gone, and my father had let his body turn lean.

My father gaped up at Jasper in horror, his face quickly morphing into one of anger I recognized all too well. Viviane grabbed my hand to pull me back further while Castor quietly moved in front of us. "Who do you think you are, stepping into family affairs like this?" my father demanded, attempting to look over their shoulders to find me.

Though I could no longer see his face, Jasper's tone was unbothered. "That is no way to talk to someone."

"Lest you forget, until she walks down that aisle, she belongs to *me*. She is *my* daughter, and I'll talk to her as I see fit," my father hissed. He clenched his fist by his side, trying and failing to control his emotions.

Regardless of the unknown life awaiting me once the wedding ended, the devil I knew was a far worse prospect.

Viviane slid between the two men, facing her brother with a look of fierce determination. "You are making a fool of yourself, Lucius," she warned. "Do not do anything you will likely regret."

As Castor moved closer to my aunt, the wedding planner burst into the foyer, snapping at someone through a headset about floral arrangements. She stopped as she glanced around the room, her face temporarily draining as she took in the tension between us. "Okay! Everyone who is not the bride, her bridesmaid, or her father must move into the chapel. We have less than two minutes until the string quartet starts up, and the processional begins!" she said, clapping her hands and ushering everyone out.

Jasper hesitated, looking between my father and me, before the planner pushed him forward and told him he needed to hurry to the adjoining room where Rion was waiting. Music drifted through the thick wooden doors before my father could make a snide comment.

I was vaguely aware of the woman speaking to us, but her words were muted as I stared straight ahead. Was I simply trading one monster for another? It was hard to say, given the little interaction I'd had with Rion, but the fact Jasper had intervened between my father and me gave me the tiniest spark of hope within my chest. My aunt was the only other person I'd ever seen do that and make it out with her head still intact.

The planner escorted Brielle into the chapel, closing the doors before I could see what awaited me on the other side. She gave me a weak smile. "Alright, you two, it's almost time! My darling Calia, if you could rest your hand on the inside of your father's elbow. And don't forget to smile!" She moved us around as if we were dolls, ensuring my hair and makeup were flawless after fluffing out my dress.

My eyes drifted close as the music blended together. The musicians played, slowly bleeding one tune into another until I had no idea where one ended, and the other had begun. The melody wasn't one I recognized, but I was already lost in the beauty of it. Somehow it grounded me, keeping my mind from wandering to dark places.

The doors opened before us, and the sound of people rising from their seats quickly followed. *This is it; there's no going back now.* I lifted my head and slowly opened my eyes, letting the scene in front of me come into focus. While I could tell everyone was dressed to the nines and the chapel was littered with beautiful flower arrangements, my gaze was quickly stolen by the man directly down the aisle from me.

Rion's dark eyes sparked with intrigue as he took me in. His fingers were interlaced in front of him, the nervous tap of his finger coinciding with each step I took toward the altar. If this had been any other situation, the way he was looking at me right now would have giddy swirls of excitement dancing in my belly.

My father and I stopped at the bottom of an elevated platform; only three small steps separated me from my future husband. The priest stepped forward, clad in long black robes that dragged along the floor. "Who gives this woman to be united with this man?" he asked, gesturing between Rion and I. His gaze was still fixed on me, making me want to shrink away.

"I do," my father said gruffly, quickly taking my hand and thrusting it into Rion's before hurrying back toward the front row of pews.

Shame threatened to heat my cheeks as I climbed the stairs, but I fought hard not to let it show. Within the hour, he would no longer hold sway over my life or decisions, and he didn't deserve the gratification of putting me down any further.

Rion's hands were cold and hard like stone, but oddly comforting. I thought he would have pulled away by now, but he kept mine in a tight grip with no hint of loosening. I slowly let my eyes drift up his body, admiring the tattoos peeking out from under his tux. He tightened his grip, pulling my attention toward his face.

Staring into his eyes was like getting lost in the night sky. Tiny flecks of silver sparkled within his obsidian gaze. I'd never seen anything like it before.

The priest began his speech—discussing the strength of unions and how they could either build this world anew or tear it to the ground. While it was a beautiful sentiment, it didn't go unnoticed that he avoided using the word 'love' at all costs. That was fine, wasn't it? After all, nothing about this had anything to do with love. Still, perhaps I wanted to bask in the thin illusion that we could, someday, find a similar quality within each other. Without it, I feared our life together would dull rapidly.

"Now is the time for the sacrament," the priest said, extending his hands. Rion took my palm and faced it toward the sky before doing the same with his own.

"Blood must be paid to appease the ancestors and seal your vow," he said, gesturing toward a golden dagger sitting on a velvet pillow next to the pew.

Rion picked it up and ran the edge of the blade against my skin before I could react. His nostrils flared as my blood welled the surface, elongating his canines to a sharp point. He brought my palm to his lips and traced the wound with his tongue. Pleasure raced through me, causing my body to arch into his until I couldn't think straight.

When he pulled away, a low moan escaped my lips as they parted. I wanted nothing more for him to quell this insatiable hunger he'd created. To soothe the fire burning in the pit of my stomach. But the spell was broken as he placed the blade in my hand, and I realized it was my turn to mark him.

I mimicked his movements, splitting open his cold skin and watching the dark red substance come to the light. Our eyes met as I bent forward and ran my tongue across his wound as he had with mine. The flavor was unexpected. The copper notes were there, but there was almost something sweet too. As I pulled away, his blood still on my lips, he reached out and wiped the remnants away with his thumb. As he placed the digit in his mouth to cleanse the spot with his tongue, I felt my inhibitions slip away.

A loud crack rang out within the cathedral, shattering the trance we found ourselves in. The screams quickly followed, sending the room into chaos. It was with a horrifying clarity that I realized they were gunshots.

I could barely breathe, especially as I looked into the eyes of our priest. Thick crimson flowed freely from his lips until his body collapsed. He lay choking on his own blood until his gaze dimmed and nothing remained but the still glaze of death.

A rigid body crashed into me, and we fell together. My name was called out, but I couldn't register the source. Someone held me down, using their body as a shield between me and the onslaught of chaos. "Please," I gasped, failing to keep my panic under control. I was hyperventilating, the edges of my vision darkening. "I...," I tried to speak, but the words felt trapped in my chest.

They leaned down and whispered in my ear as their weight lifted slightly. "Breathe," they commanded.

I fought for air, but no matter how hard I tried, I couldn't take enough into my lungs. The smell of blood was overwhelming, and I couldn't help but stare into the dead priest's eyes as I spiraled downward. "I—I can't." Glass shattered from above, sending sharp shards raining down on us. I narrowly covered my head in time, but didn't miss the keen sting of cuts along my fingers.

I was going to die.

Would anyone other than my aunt's family mourn me? I hardly had friends due to my introverted nature and my overbearing father. People would come to my funeral, weeping for a tragic life lost too soon. But I would be forgotten by the time the sun set on the day.

The person above me reached over, intertwining their fingers with mine and placing them on the floor. "*Breathe!*" they commanded again, their tone sharp and laced with authority. This time my body succumbed to their command. On the next inhale, I felt a rush of air filling my lungs. The darkness abated with each breath, and I grounded myself with the thundering beat of this person's heart.

It took a moment for me to realize the shooting had stopped, though the sounds still rang in my mind. People were still shouting, and I heard feet crunching against the glass. "Calia! Calia!" This time I recognized the voice calling out for me, and I struggled underneath the body still covering my own.

The world spun as I pushed off the ground, and I reached out for something to steady me before I lost my footing. Rough hands gripped my own, and I looked up into Rion's cold face. His depthless eyes, which had been black only moments ago, were now an icy silver that glittered with untethered power. "T—Thank you," I stammered, pulling away from his hold.

He dipped his chin, stepping back as Brielle and my aunt barreled into me. They pulled me in tightly, only pulling back to check me for injuries. I could barely concentrate on their words, refusing to lose Rion in the crowd. The guests fled during the shootout, leaving only those closest to us lingering to inspect the damage.

My father stood, brushing a piece of fallen hair out of his face as he surveyed the few dead bodies around us. His spiteful gaze landed on Rion, but before he could open his mouth to spew his venom, the heavy doors of the chapel burst open. I watched as my uncle and Jasper stalked through the room, a man hanging limply between them. He let out small sobs and pleas for mercy, begging everyone for help, but his cries elicited no pity. As they drew near, Jasper forced the man down on his knees at Rion's feet while my uncle approached and kissed my forehead.

"Please, please, please," the man whimpered. "I was set up! I was—"

Jasper held the man in place as Rion bent down and gripped him by the throat, cutting off both his oxygen and his words in one quick strike. "Who sent you, human?" he asked, voice low and lethal. Goosebumps skittered across my flesh as I watched him inhale deeply. Growing up, we'd been told vampyres could taste a lie with a single drop of blood. It was a story that began as a cautionary tale, but seeing Rion work in front of me, I couldn't help but wonder if there might be any truth to it.

The man fought against their hold, his face turning blue as Rion finally released his grip. "I don't know who it was," he gasped. "I only answered the hit. It was untraceable."

Rion looked at Jasper as the human's head sagged, a small trickle of blood running down his chin. Apprehension ran down my spine as they silently communicated, occasionally glancing up at me. "Who was the target?"

The man said nothing as we waited on bated breath

to hear a name. Instead, he shook his head vigorously, looking up into my eyes. "You're not safe with any of these creatures," he rasped. "They will use you until you are spent."

My aunt's grip tightened on my bicep, but I was too shocked to say anything. Was he referring to the D'Arcy family, or perhaps even my own? Before I could question him, Rion moved with lightning speed. His hand plunged into the man's chest, a snarl crossing his face as he leaned in close to watch the light die from his prey's eyes.

His excitement was palpable, fangs peeking out from under his top lip, but he paused before leaning in and staring at me. I was frozen in shock, immobilized by fear and a shameful desire to know what they would feel like scraping against my neck and—

Rion pulled his hand free from the man's body with a wet pop. Hot, sticky blood splattered against my face and chest, seeping through the fabric of my dress and staining my skin. He clutched the man's heart in his palm before letting it fall from his fingertips to the floor at my feet.

This was a test, one I was trying not to fail. I felt every eye on me, gauging my reaction until I felt anxiety rush to the surface. But I refused to shy away from these people—especially Rion. Had he done it to scare me? To show me who he was beneath it all? He was underestimating me if he assumed a little murder would send me running. He was wrong.

While my mother was alive, she shielded me from

my father's depraved nature, but once she was gone, he'd force me to watch as he carved up those who had wronged him. It was a lesson—he told me—a reminder that even if I disappointed him, I still had the Darrow name, and Darrows never let those wrongs go unpunished.

Rion's mother came up behind him, tsking as she looked down at the body. "What a waste," she said with a sigh. Her eyes followed the trail of blood from the floor up to my face, widening in hunger as she stepped forward and dragged a single digit through the mess across my cheek. "Welcome to the family," she said with a wolfish grin, before licking her finger clean.

five

I sat next to Rion in the back of a sleek black town car, the silence near suffocating. After what happened in the cathedral, there'd been no time to think, let alone catch my breath. Rion's mother insisted we continue as if nothing had happened, not even giving me a moment to wipe the smeared blood from my face.

The body of our dead priest was removed, so I didn't have to stand over his corpse as Rion and I pledged ourselves to one another. His blood, on the other hand, stained the bottom of my gown and smeared across the marble flooring as I made my way out of the chapel.

Dark water rippled past us as the car drove across the bridge toward Rion's home. I'd seen the imposing, gothic mansion before—usually, during early morning strolls along the banks of the Odesza. I was always curious to know what secrets were held behind its massive walls. Now, I was only moments from finding out, and I wasn't sure if I was still as curious as I used to be.

He checked the time on his watch before turning toward the window with a soft sigh. His foot tapped gently against the floorboard, almost muted by the soft piano music flowing from the speakers. "We're almost there, sir," the driver said. When Rion didn't respond, I glanced out the windshield for a better view.

Straight ahead was an imposing wrought-iron gate; sharp points lined the top, preventing birds from perching atop it. It nearly reached the branches of tall hemlock trees lining the drive. With the press of a button, the gate swung open to reveal a winding drive. Tall spires peeked out from atop the small surrounding forest, letting the last glint of sunlight against the glass beam down on us.

In front of the house was a large circular driveway encompassing a great black fountain. In the middle stood a marble goddess with her hands outstretched, her head tilted to the sky in prayer. "Beautiful," I muttered, unable to pull myself away from looking at her.

Was it pain or pleasure written across her face? Did she have a name, or was she cursed to remain unknown until she crumbled away?

As the car came to a stop, Rion cleared his throat. "Excuse us for a moment, Hendrix." The driver stepped out and stood near the back of the car. The night was approaching, and the windows were tinted so dark it was hard to see. When Rion turned to me, I straightened my posture ever so slightly. "Under different circumstances, we would have been able to speak about this beforehand, but there was no time, given the nature of our agreement. We will go over my expectations in the morning—"

"*Expectations*?" I echoed, biting back a laugh. When his face showed no hint of joking, I paused. "I'm not a child to be managed. I understand how to act and can do so without supervision."

"Not within my society. And as you are my wife, you will need to be ready for anything."

"Believe me, I understand the expectations of being married to a man like you. No matter what you are, you're all the same." The day's exhaustion wore heavy on my body, and I couldn't hold back my frustrations.

His hand shot out and gripped my chin tightly, pulling me forward until we shared breaths. He looked down at me as though he could crush me beneath his feet, but some part of that excited me. It made me want to fight—to push back and see how far I could take this.

His gaze landed on my lips, lingering momentarily before his stormy eyes met mine. "I will say this once, and *only* once. Tread lightly with that wicked tongue, Calia. We have an eternity together; it would be a shame to lose it so quickly." His cool fingertips had the opposite effect, lighting my skin on fire where he touched. When I said nothing, he continued. "This evening will be intimate—family only—but that does not mean they will not test you to find your weaknesses. If you think you have none, think again. The smallest tick could be your downfall."

He spoke as if my ruin was already set in stone. Maybe it was. The prospect should have been more terrifying than it was, but I couldn't focus on anything else when he held me in his grip. I wasn't afraid of dying; I was afraid of not living. And I didn't know if I wanted to live without knowing how it felt to be used by him just once.

"How would you like me to act, then? What would be suitable for you, *husband*?"

Rion's jaw flexed, eyes burning with a ferocity I'd never seen. Quickly, he let me go, and I fell forward in his touch's absence. Heat bloomed across my cheeks, and when he saw it, a smug smirk stretched across his lips that only fueled the quiet rage burning inside me.

"Oh, love," he muttered, tapping on the glass. The door immediately opened, Hendrix pulling it wide and offering a hand for me to take. "There are many things that would suit me, but most would make a blush creep across your pretty face."

Cool air brushed against my skin, and I closed my eyes against the emotions threatening to spill over. My nipples ached against the fabric of my stained wedding dress, especially as he stood tall before me and buttoned his suit jacket. A hard hand brushed against my arm, and I took it without question as we ascended the marble steps toward the imposing arched door. Thick lines of glimmering black metal ran down panes of frosted glass, illuminated by softly glowing light.

The doors swung open, revealing an expansive foyer. Above our heads, a matte black chandelier inlaid with sapphires flickered with warm lights, casting a glow down on worn hardwood floors. Cedar and vanilla filled my nostrils, a warm and inviting scent enveloping me in nostalgia. I couldn't recall the familiarity, only that it grounded me.

"Hendrix will show you to your room. You'll have one hour until dinner." His eyes scanned my body, lingering along my collarbones and neck. "Clean yourself up," he grumbled, leaving me alone, listening to his footsteps echoing down the hall.

six

Fifty-nine minutes later, after I'd spent most of it scrubbing blood from my skin, I found Jasper leaning against the wall outside my room. He smiled when he saw me, offering his elbow for me to take. Neither of us spoke as he escorted me through the manor and into the dining room. We were the last to arrive, Jasper silently guiding me to the seat next to Rion before taking his spot across the table.

My husband was at the head of the table, a large tumbler of whiskey sat in front of him. From the other side, my aunt and uncle eyed everyone with careful regard. They gave me a subtle smile as I took my seat, smoothing out the thin velvet dress laid out for me.

Quiet conversations carried on around me, but I paid them no mind. Brielle and I chatted, talking about anything but what happened today. Rion spoke to an older man with peppered hair. An angry purple scar ran across his neck, drawing attention away from the scowl that seemed permanently etched upon his face. Occasionally, my father glared at me from beside my aunt, but I refused to acknowledge him. He had no sway on my life after today.

Servers came and went, placing decadent meals before us while others refilled crystal goblets with a viscous red liquid. As everyone began to eat, Leonora cleared her throat, gripping her glass with a tight-lipped smile. "Thank you all for coming this evening."

Her words were met with polite, half-hearted applause. No one here believed what she said, but if it made them feel better, who was I to judge? The man beside Rion smirked, raking his eyes over me as if I were a meal. "Well, we are all a part of this farce, are we not?" He held up his glass, in the light I saw it for what it was— thick, crimson blood.

Leonora's eyes sparkled as she laughed. "Come now, Renwick. This is not the time to discuss such matters."

"If not now, when?" he countered, leaning forward on the table. The tension in the room drew tight as every person turned his way. His prominent eyebrows drew together as he sighed. "Is the point of this not to move forward for the better of our society? And does that not include seeing that our people are adequately cared for? We've been cast aside and treated like rabid animals for too long. We cannot even step out in the sun without dying."

My father, unwilling to waste an opportunity to speak his mind, raised his wine to his lips. He chuckled before taking a drink. "I would think your midnight strolls are enough to keep your thirst abated, Renwick. The latest string of human disappearances was, after all, in your district, were they not?"

"Lucius," my aunt warned, clasping Castor's hand atop the table as she swiveled her head toward my father. Brielle did the same to me, finding my clammy hand and squeezing it below the table.

I knew that glint in my father's eye, the one that swam with disdain and promised retribution. It didn't help that he'd been guzzling bourbon all evening. Even from here, I could smell the way it lingered on his breath from across the room.

"And how many vampyres have your men murdered in the streets within the past month?" Renwick snarled, the grip on his temper snapping. I'd never met someone with the same short fuse as my father, but given the fury radiating from his body, I feared he'd met his match. "Your ancestor is at fault for this *union*." He said the word as though it tasted sour on his tongue. "He cursed us all because he refused to share power, and his actions have continued to damn our children. Your daughter will never be worthy of our family." He threw a shaky finger in my direction, his lip curling as he let loose a vicious snarl.

I felt every ounce of his hatred, and what surprised me the most was how I felt my own rising inside my chest. I wanted to tear his hand from his body and watch as he screamed. I'd never felt anything like it before, and even the thought made me uneasy. —

"*Our* ancestors? We are not the ones who—"

"*Quiet!*" Rion's voice boomed across the table. The authority in his tone had me clasping my lips together even though I'd barely said a word all evening. All thoughts eddied away from my mind until I felt empty, the rage floating away like dandelion seeds in the wind. He stood, dark eyes traveling along the length of the room. Every person in attendance seemed to react, shrinking away from his stormy gaze. "The union between Calia and I is done. We are married, and there is no way around it."

"You're damn right. There is no going back," my father grumbled. "Contracts have been signed, and she has been delivered."

I closed my eyes as Renwick laughed. "Is that why you were willing to let her go without much thought? Because the bitch holds such little value to you?"

My uncle slammed his fist down on the table, causing the wood to quake. "Watch your fucking mouth."

"Oh, have I struck a nerve, Castor?" Renwick asked, a disgusting smirk stretching across his lips.

Around and around, the insults were tossed as if I wasn't sitting at the table. Heat bloomed in my cheeks, and I wished the room would swallow me whole. Rion remained quiet throughout the exchange, using the time to study my father with interest. He cocked his head to the side before resting it upon his hand. "That is your daughter—your blood. You dare dismiss her so casually?"

My father snorted. "It matters not to me. She's no longer my concern. What you do with her is your problem," he said, leaning back in his chair. He swept his napkin across his lips and threw it atop his plate.

Rion moved fast, sidling up behind me before I could blink. I hadn't known he had placed a blade against my neck until the metal dug into my skin. My aunt cried out as my uncle wrapped an arm around her, eyes wide as they observed the dinner knife along the tender skin of my throat. Brielle clasped her hand over her mouth in horror.

"So, you would not care if I slit her throat before you and drained her of her life? If every vampyre here feasted upon her flesh? The way she smells..." I shivered as he slid my hair over my shoulder and ran his nose along my neck. "One taste would not be enough. We would devour her until there was nothing left, pull every last drop of blood from her body."

Every word from his mouth should have repulsed me, and in some part, it did. But another, secret part wanted to know what it would be like to feel the scrape of his fangs as they broke my skin once more—if he was allowed unrestricted access to my blood. Would he truly kill me? Would it be drawn out or quick?

Did I care?

"Lucius, stop this madness," my aunt begged before turning her pleading eyes toward Rion. "I–*We* care for Calia. Deeply. Regardless of what my useless brother says or does not, she is loved and cared for by us, and if you so much as harm—"

Castor reached for the gun I knew he always carried, concealed or not, and aimed it at my father's head. "If I kill him here and now, will that temper the insult he's laid upon you and your family?"

My father raised his hands, sweat dripping down his temple as he laughed nervously. There were reasons he hated Castor as much as he did, but he was also terrified of my uncle. Castor could kill him before he even batted an eye. "I believe this has been blown out of proportion, D'Arcy," he said, nodding toward the gun Castor held in his hand. "Perhaps my words were too harsh—"

"Get out," Rion growled, letting the knife clatter to the dinner plate before stepping away from my chair. I let out a shaky breath, steeling myself. It took every bit of effort I had not to run from the room and cower, but I knew better than to take off in a room full of predators.

Especially now that Rion had drawn attention to my scent.

Jasper stood from the table. His golden eyes seemed to glow in the dim lighting, goosebumps flaring along my skin. As he stepped toward my father, I noticed his hand on his pistol as he scanned the room.

He reached out to grab my father, but the coward nearly knocked his chair to the ground in his attempt to escape. He said nothing as he stormed past Jasper, nor did he spare me a last glance before he fled. Every soul was quiet, even Renwick, who suddenly seemed content to sip his refreshments with a furrowed brow.

Castor sat, but instead of placing the gun back where it had been tucked away, he placed it on the table within reach. No one said a word. Even amongst the vampyres, he was offered a level of respect many others weren't. He kissed my aunt's temple before leveling a stare at my new husband. "I don't mean to tell you what to do in your own home," he said, sitting back in his chair. "But if you ever threaten my niece's life like that again, I'll ensure you spend the rest of yours regretting the day you laid a hand upon her. Is that clear?"

Rion's chair scraped against the floor as he pulled it out and sunk into the plush fabric. Reaching forward, he grabbed the glass of whiskey before him and quickly downed it before grimacing and meeting my uncle's glare. "Crystal."

seven

The rest of the evening passed by without further theatrics. Though awkward at first, our dinner ended with laughter and jovial cheers once our bellies were filled to the brim with exquisite food. As the clock struck two, I realized just how long the night had been. My aunt and uncle wrapped their arms around me tightly before departing. Brielle followed, making me promise to meet her for coffee within the week to hear all about the sordid details of my wedding night before pressing my mother's picture into my hand.

I'd have nothing to divulge, but I kept that detail to myself.

My stomach dropped as the door closed behind them. I already missed the warmth I felt in their presence as I stood in the middle of the cavernous foyer with my arm wrapped around myself, wondering where to go from here.

The click of shoes against tile had me spinning around, staring up into Rion's unblinking gaze. "Do you need me to show you to your room?" he murmured.

I searched for any trace of coldness in his tone, but found none. Instead, I lingered along the deep frown line between his brow and the way his eyes were a polychromatic pit of greys and blacks. They were unlike anything I'd ever seen—a reminder of the old films my mother loved once upon a time.

It seemed that Rion rarely showed emotion. Everything he did was calculated—each action had an explicit purpose—and he didn't waste time on anything that wouldn't benefit or interest him.

"Calia?" he asked, pulling me from my thoughts.

I ducked my head, composing myself. "That would be great. I wasn't paying attention earlier when Hendrix showed me."

"And why is that?"

We slowly made our way up the curving staircase leading to the second story of his home. The beautiful, deep green walls reminded me of the forest outstretched along the isle. The color carried throughout the hallways, accented with black crown molding and the smallest glints of gold.

"Have you seen this place?" I asked, taking in the tall ceilings above us. "It's breathtaking."

Rion said nothing as we ambled along the corridor. Still, the occasional prick of awareness along my skin told me he was watching. We stopped near the bottom of a smaller staircase which wound up to the third floor. Or perhaps it led to the tall tower which proudly stood watch over the Odesza.

I'd never been fond of heights, but something about that tower intrigued me. I'd always admired the architecture when I was in Kallistos, wanting to know just how far I could see out over the land and to watch the subtle waves across the river as the wind blew.

No matter how unsure I was of what my new life would entail, I knew I'd be able to find solace in small moments such as those.

"What's up there?" I asked, allowing my curiosity to get the best of me.

"Nothing that concerns you," he said, reaching for my elbow and softly tugging me toward him.

My brows furrowed. "And why not?"

"Because I said so. You can move about the house however you'd like, but not there."

"So, I'm expected to live in a home I can't explore?"

"Let's cut the bullshit, shall we?" He sighed, and I realized it was the closest I'd seen to emotion. "I am a private man, Calia, and I would like to maintain a semblance of that privacy, even in marriage. One, I will remind you, neither of us had a say in. I would respect your wishes if you bar me from your rooms. Can you not do the same for mine?"

His request was reasonable, and given this was our first night together, I didn't want to test the limits of his patience. "Fine."

He said nothing as he led me the remainder of the

way, stopping in front of a large wooden door I recognized. When he pushed it open, I walked inside, awestruck by the decadence dripping from the soft cream-colored walls.

There'd been such little time to take it all in when I'd changed earlier, but now that I was here, I paused. Everything in this room stood in opposition to what I'd seen of Rion's home so far. It was light and airy, with windows overlooking the Odesza. Glass doors opened to a small balcony with a deep-set blue velvet armchair I wanted to fall into with a book. A large canopy bed dominated the space, piled with deep jewel-toned pillows that gave the room a stunning pop of color while tying it to the décor of the rest of the house.

He rested against the door frame, watching me as I ran my finger along a dresser filled with brand-new clothing. "So, this will be our room?"

I couldn't stop myself from asking the question as I turned to look at him. It seemed innocent enough, especially now that we were married. Wasn't that the point of the arrangement? To unite our people by way of blood and marriage?

Rion's jaw clenched tightly as he shook his head. "No. This is your room and yours alone. I will stay in my own."

I nodded my head. "Okay."

As if he wanted to drive his point home, he continued as if I hadn't spoken. "We will be married in name only, living separate lives in the comfort of my home."

"You can't be serious?" I asked, quirking a brow.

He pushed off the wall and stalked forward until I could only stare straight at him. I was tall for a female, but Rion towered over me. The energy shifted between us in warning. "What did you expect, love?" he growled, pushing a lock of hair behind my ear and causing goose-bumps to pebble along my flesh. "Did you think I would share a magical evening together with the woman whose family damned my own?"

I narrowed my eyes at his jab. Frankly, I was sick to death of listening to the insults intended toward my family. The insults berated me my entire life. But some-how, the words coming from him instead of some random stranger had my anger rising. "You've conveniently left out the part where my ancestor had no choice given the bloodlust of *your* people. And regard-less of what has happened in the past, I haven't done anything but try to make the best out of a situation neither of us asked to be a part of. The least you could do is recognize that."

We stood nose-to-nose, neither of us backing down from the sharp cracks splitting our union already. It hadn't even been a full day, which was a joke. If we couldn't make it twenty-four hours, how the hell were we supposed to make it a lifetime? Finally, Rion spoke. "This was an arrangement. Nothing more. You're free to live how you see fit, given you reside here, and I will do the same. When we are required to make public appear-ances, I will be the perfect doting husband, but make no mistake... That is where it ends."

His cruel words brought me back to our conversation, and suddenly I allowed my anger to dominate my body. "What am I supposed to do, then? Twiddle my thumbs while you're out doing gods only know what with whoever you want?"

He dropped his shoulders and straightened to his full height. "Frankly, I don't care what you do as long as you keep it private."

There was no malice in his words, just calm indifference. For some reason, that hurt me more than anything. I wanted him to feel *something*, to understand how ridiculous it was to rip me from one prison, only to place me in another. "So, I could bring a man into this house, fuck him wherever I please until I screamed his name, and you would be fine with that?"

"Whatever you do in private is your business. I have no plans to stay abstinent. It would be quite the double standard for me to hold you to the same outdated notion." He leaned in once more, his breath fanning against my cheek. "So, do as you please, Calia. Just as long as you remember, either way, you still belong to me."

With that declaration, he left me standing slack-jawed in the middle of the room, craving something I knew I shouldn't want and would never have.

eight

Sweat dripped along my back, the blue silk nightgown sticking to my skin as I bolted upright. My heart thrummed beneath my hand as I laid in on my chest, willing the muscle to slow before it gave out. "It was just a nightmare," I whispered to myself, taking a deep breath. "Just a nightmare."

Now and then, my mother's face would slip into my dreams. What would start as a lovely memory would morph into the cruelest torture as a figure shrouded in darkness took her away from me. I was forced to listen to her screams fade into choked sobs until she eventually grew silent. Then the figure would turn to me, their dark, malice-filled eyes twinkling from the shadows.

I always awakened before they reached me.

Pushing out of bed, I padded softly across the old wooden floor to the adjoining bathroom. A small, flickering lantern lit the space softly, guiding me to the mirror.

Turning the handle, cold water rushed from the faucet. I bent forward, trapping the liquid before splashing it over my face to wash away the sweat left behind. It didn't clear the horrible images from my mind, but nothing would.

There would be no more sleep for me tonight.

I turned off the water and grabbed a towel. It smelled like Rion—sensual, old, and expensive—like a rare book. Of course, I couldn't escape him even for a moment. Not even in what was supposed to be my own space.

Why was I so bothered by someone who wanted nothing to do with me? Our situation could've been worse. He could have decided to imprison me, keeping me entirely isolated. Instead, Rion honestly didn't seem to care what I did with my free time if I kept it private.

That *should* be a good thing.

Right?

"I have no plans to stay abstinent." That's what he'd said, verbatim. So, why was the thought of him doing just that causing my skin to crawl?

Instead of moving back toward my bed, I reached the door and placed my ear against the wood. *Silence.* The clock on my nightstand read just past three in the morning. It wouldn't be long until that peace was replaced with a household rife with discontent at my arrival.

But if I went out now, got a snack and some coffee, I

could hide here a little longer. Maybe they would forget about me entirely.

I grabbed my robe and stepped outside, looking down the halls to ensure there wasn't anyone lurking in the darkness. I wouldn't put it past Rion to station guards outside my door. Vampyres had the ability to conceal themselves in the shadows, ensuring prying eyes went unseeing. As they hunted, they could stalk their prey without detection,

Wandering downstairs, I trailed my finger along the thick wooden banister as I went. The space was illuminated by sconces that looked like they didn't belong in this century, but somehow, they matched the room perfectly. Their dim light was just enough to guide me to the first floor.

Shit. I had no idea where the kitchen was, and I'd been too wrapped up in Rion's suffocating presence to ask. But how hard could it be to find? The dining room we'd been in only hours ago sat empty, and I vaguely remembered a set of doors where the servers had gone in and out. Surely that would lead me *somewhere*.

Before I could walk toward them, soft footsteps sounded from up ahead. I fixed my gaze on the darkening hallway, knowing I'd likely be met with more questions than answers.

"Hello?" I called, tightening my hand into a fist at my side.

"Can't sleep?" a deep voice called before stepping out of the shadows into the dim foyer. Jasper stood before me, hair mussed and bare-chested in soft linen sleep pants. A single snake tattoo ran across his chest and down his left arm.

Holy gods.

I shifted on my feet, trying desperately not to stare at the carved lines of muscle disappearing below his pajamas. *Stop. Stop. Stop.* "Yeah, I always have trouble in a new place. I was on the hunt to find the kitchen, but—"

"But you have no idea where you're going?"

I chuckled. "I might be a bit lost, yeah."

His amber eyes glittered, especially as he pulled a cookie from behind his back and took a bite. "Lucky for you, I was just on a similar endeavor. Want me to show you where all the best treats are hidden?"

I nodded, moving toward him. "You keep them hidden?"

"Rion has a sweet tooth, believe it or not. It is something he has developed."

"Developed?" I asked, wondering what would make such a dour vampyre crave something so seemingly normal.

Jasper winced slightly. "To curb his...other cravings."

Right. Because he was a vampyre, and the one thing he *truly* craved was blood.

"Ah," I said, keeping my head down. I focused on the feeling of the cold floor beneath my feet, but nothing took away the image conjuring in my mind of Rion lengthening his fangs and—

"I didn't make you uncomfortable, did I?" Jasper asked as we rounded the corner, stepping into the spacious kitchen area.

Dark jade cabinets were paired with gold accents, the counters a black so glossy I could nearly see my reflection. There was a lighter honeycomb backsplash along the wall below the cabinets.

"Calia?" Jasper prompted when I said nothing. He opened the large fridge and pulled out a gallon of milk, which he poured into a saucepan to heat.

I tucked my hair behind my ear and seated myself on a velvet stool. "Uh, no. Not at all. I'm just not used to the...blood talk. I guess it'll take some getting used to." Which was putting it mildly, at best. Even when vampyres and their feeding habits were discussed as I was growing up, it was always seen as an evil act—that they were attempting to drain away the life and power of everyone around them.

Jasper turned his back to me before reaching for a mug and pouring the heated liquid. "Do you like chocolate?"

"Only the dark kind. I made myself sick on the regular stuff when I was a kid and haven't been able to look at it the same." My mom and I had stayed up late to watch a movie, one I'd begged her to watch with me even though we'd both seen it a million times. I'd gorged myself on every candy bar I could find and threw up for the rest of the evening.

He smiled briefly before walking to the pantry and reaching for something on the top shelf. I couldn't help but stare, watching his muscles contract as he extended his body. It should have been illegal to look that damn good, but here he was in front of me in all his glory.

He's not who you should be staring at, my mind scolded. I looked away before he caught me, though I felt the blush heat my cheeks. He said nothing if he noticed, but I'm sure he did.

Jasper turned and slid a cup across the counter to me. It was fresh hot chocolate, complete with whipped cream and chocolate shavings. The rich, dark aroma filled my nostrils, and I had to bite my lip to keep myself from groaning.

"I hope you like it," he said, making another for himself. "It's my specialty."

I took a sip, savoring the flavor dancing across my tongue. "Not much of a cook, huh?"

He shook his head. "Gods, no. I burn bread. But this recipe has stayed with me since I was a child, and I would like to think it makes up for my lack of culinary skills."

Jasper walked over and sat beside me, watching me closely as I held the mug close to my lips. "Do you always make this for women you find wandering around the house at five in the morning?"

He tossed his head back in laughter, wrinkles creasing the skin around his eyes. "I may have tried it a time or two before, but it has never been quite like this."

I held up my mug and clinked it against his. "I respect your tactics, sir. They are certainly effective." Jasper momentarily stilled at my words, and I realized what I'd said too late. "Not that I mean to imply you were hitting on me! That would be inappropriate, and there's nothing inappropriate about sharing hot cocoa with my new husband's bodyguard."

My eyes snapped close as I wished I was anywhere but here, especially as he laughed. *Jeez, Calia. Real fucking smooth.*

"*Technically*," he drawled, "I'm *your* bodyguard for now." I lifted one lid to see him smiling back at me. He leaned over and bumped my shoulder. "And for the record, I knew what you meant. But I couldn't resist watching you dig yourself into a bit of a hole."

"You ass!" I yelled, smacking his shoulder with the back of my hand. "That was embarrassing!"

"Only for you. I quite enjoyed it," he joked, reaching forward and swiping a glob of rich cream from his mug and popping it in his mouth.

"Am I interrupting something, *wife*?"

nine

R ion's voice fell over me like a bucket of ice water, chilling me on the deepest level. Especially as I turned around to see his seething gaze flicking between the small space separating me and his best friend.

"Fucking vampyres," I muttered, hating their stealth. Living with them would be harder than I thought.

Jasper didn't move, but I pushed away as if we were doing something wrong. Which was silly, I knew that, but I could also admit there was something not entirely innocent in the way Jasper looked at me, nor in how *I* felt when he did so.

What was it about him that had butterflies flitting around in my stomach? I knew nothing about him and had barely spoken to him for more than an hour, but I felt comfortable with him around, nevertheless.

But now, I wanted to be as far away from him as

possible. I should never have left my room; I should have trusted that first inkling that I wasn't alone. But I'd never listened to my gut, no matter how badly I needed to.

Jasper shrugged his shoulder and brought the mug to his lips for one last gulp, staring directly at his friend. "Not at all, Rion. I found poor Calia wandering about this large house earlier." He drew his eyebrows together, conveying a silent message to his friend I wasn't privy to before leaning back on the stool. "She didn't know where the kitchen was since she wasn't given a tour."

"I was going to give her one this morning. I assumed she had everything she needed when we parted ways last night." Rion responded, his voice tight. "If I had known she wanted one before I retired, I would have done so myself."

"I couldn't sleep," I said, offering no further explanation. Rion didn't care if nightmares kept me awake every night, that they were filled with demons with no faces, and there was no sense in bothering him about my past. Even if the way he was studying me had me wondering if he knew about it anyway. "And I didn't want to spend my time staring up at my ceiling, waiting for the sun to rise, so I decided to find something to occupy my time. We ran into each other in the foyer, and Jasper was kind enough to help me."

Rion's posture straightened as he crossed his arms over his broad chest. He looked like he'd never gone to sleep; the top three buttons on his white shirt were unbuttoned, the beginning of a deep scar barely visible.

His hair was tousled, looking like hands had been running through it for hours. Had they been his own? Or had he already occupied his time with another woman?

"Go back to bed, Calia," Rion growled. "You have a long day ahead of you."

I opened my mouth to object, but Jasper intercepted and placed a hand between my shoulders. Rion tracked the movement, but if he cared, he didn't show it. Disappointment coursed through me as I tried to figure out why I wanted him to in the first place. "Come, Calia. Let me walk you back," he said, offering a listless smile.

"Sure," I whispered, letting Jasper move me past Rion. His hand shot out to grip my arm when I tried to side-step him, forcing me to stop. We lingered in a stalemate which forced us to either clear the air or allow the tension to build. He opened his mouth, and I waited for a cutting remark that never came. Instead, he cleared his throat and moved to the side to let us pass. "Goodnight, Calia."

The absence of his words told me everything I needed to know.

Jasper nudged me forward, and I didn't object as he guided us out of the kitchen. The silence stretched between us as we trudged up the stairs and back toward my room.

"Will it always be like this?" I asked Jasper as we stood outside my door. I looked up at him, knowing he was the closest thing to a friend or ally I had here. Even if he was the right-hand of the devil.

Jasper paused, cocking his head to the side. "What do you mean?"

Instinctively, I wrapped myself in a hug, seeking comfort no one else could provide. "You know what I mean. Rion hates me, and don't deny it because it's written on his face every time he looks at me. You know, it's not like I chose this. I don't want it any more than he does."

Emotions I didn't want to think about sharpened their claws in preparation to fight their way to the surface. This was no way to live; I didn't want to spend my life walking on eggshells with a man who carelessly crushed everything beneath his feet. But fate was, frankly, a bitch. I had no other choice.

"He already told me he has no plans of changing how he leads his life—the women, the parties, whatever. Don't get me wrong, I had zero expectations of us falling in love and living happily ever after, but I expected *something* dammit." My voice faltered as I fought to keep my rising emotions at bay.

These were the moments I craved my mother's love. To know that despite whatever happened, I would be okay. But I hadn't felt comfort like that since she died, despite my aunt generously attempting to ensure I never went without. Nothing had been the same since I woke to the sound of sirens and pained screams echoing through the house.

"Calia," Jasper whispered, taking hold of my hand and running his thumb across my skin.

I shook my head furiously, tugging out of his grip. "I don't want your pity, Jasper."

He studied me under furrowed brows, undoubtedly contemplating what to say that wouldn't have me locking myself away and never coming out again, before he spoke. "Look, I cannot pretend to understand the extent of the animosity between your families, but you are not just a spectator, Calia. You hear me? You are something special—a key component to fixing the fucked-up status between our people. And Rion knows that, but he is horrible at showing it." Jasper placed his large hand on my shoulder, his touch lingering before he pulled away. "It will get better. I promise."

It was easy for someone on the outside looking in to believe that, but I wasn't so sure. "How can you promise something like that?"

"Because I will beat the shit out of him if it doesn't," he said with a smile.

I couldn't help but laugh, letting the tension I'd been holding onto roll off. "I don't think you're allowed to do that."

"I have been his friend longer than I have been in his employ. I'm entitled to some job perks, and this happens to be one of them," he said, shrugging. "Now try and get some more sleep. I have a feeling he will call soon just to be an ass and will not let you rest until you have memorized every inch of this isle."

Jasper had been right.

Not even an hour later, there was a knock on my door, and a large, folded paper slid under the opening. I hadn't gone back to sleep, instead curling up on the armchair on the balcony as the sun rose into the sky. The air was so much clearer than in the city, even though I could see the skyscrapers from across the lake.

It might have actually been beautiful if it wasn't tainted by a D'Arcy sized dark cloud hanging over my head.

I walked over to where the note lay and unfolded it. Something I regretted as soon as I did. Someone, and I had a decent idea who, had drawn a map leading from my bedroom to the kitchen.

In case you get lost.

– R

Arrogant ass.

It didn't take long to get ready, slipping on a pair of jeans and a T-shirt before snatching the note off my dresser and heading to the kitchen. I rounded the corner, instantly halting as I sensed his presence.

The bane of my existence was sitting against a small breakfast nook in the corner, the connecting panes of frosted glass and thick metal grilles which created a golden aura haloing his figure. He seemed more like a god than a monster, and for just one moment, I didn't stop myself from staring.

Dark hair curled around the nape of his neck, still wet from a shower. His broad shoulders took up most of the space on the other side of the table as he fingered the rim of his coffee cup. He wore a navy button-down shirt that was tucked into heather grey slacks. Both were fitted to his body with extreme precision and left no mystery to the physique he had underneath.

He paused, turning toward the windows. The muted light danced across his face as he closed his eyes. For just a moment, I saw a glimpse of a man I wanted to know. Did he wish to step into the sun like the rest of society? Did he feel a disconnect in his soul like I did by not being able to be amongst the stars?

"It is not polite to stare, you know," he mused, focusing his gaze back on the tablet in front of him. "But I am feeling generous, so please continue."

Did I say I wanted to get to know him? Because I've changed my mind.

I approached the counter, staring at the fancy coffee machine near the stove. "How do you work this thing?"

"I have absolutely no idea," he drawled, taking a long sip from his mug.

Fine. If he wanted to be a smug bastard, he was entitled to do so. But if he thought it would get a rise out of me, he was mistaken. Even if my only reason was to keep the moral high ground. That would quickly crumble if I couldn't figure out how to work this damn machine. After nearly five minutes of pressing buttons and turning dials, I began to smell the bitter aroma I craved.

"Congratulations. You are smarter than a machine."

My hands clenched around the marble countertop as I pursed my lips. Gods above, he was an ass. An utter, inconsiderate ass that I was now married to. For better or worse, and until death do us part. That didn't mean I couldn't give as well as I could take.

I turned around, pasting a saccharine smile on my face. "How did you sleep, darling husband?"

"I didn't," he said, setting the tablet down and leveling me with an unamused look. "But you already knew that."

"I did not," I began before he raised his eyebrows, my shoulders slumping. "It's called polite conversation, Rion. Look it up."

"Can't say I am a fan."

I brought my coffee to my lips, savoring the taste and smell. "Are you a fan of anything?" I muttered to myself before turning around and taking a sip. Getting through to him would be more complicated than I thought, but I liked the challenge. Eventually, I would break his icy shield, and instead of this cold, bitter banter, he might see me as a friend.

"*No.*" Goosebumps prickled against my skin as I felt his presence behind me, lips skimming the sensitive skin along my ear. Hot breath fanned the back of my neck, and I couldn't stop myself from closing my eyes as his arms caged me in on either side.

"I forgot how fast vampyres could move," I murmured, fighting to control my erratic heart. My experience with Rion's people was limited at best. I'd only ever met one, which happened to be my husband's father. My memory was hazy on the events; I'd been so little, but I remember Ramsey as a kind soul.

Rion let loose a deep chuckle. "Do not forget the exceptional hearing, too." He dropped his voice lower. "It is hard to have private conversations in this kitchen without being overheard." As I faced him, he pulled back and leaned against the island opposite me. One long leg crossed the other as his hands slid into the pockets of his slacks. "Such as ones you have early in the morning with my bodyguard in my house—"

"*Our* house," I said, correcting him. He cocked an eyebrow, clearly unamused at my declaration. "You said it was your house, but this is *our* house. I live here now, too."

"It is *my* family home," he argued, widening his stance.

I smirked before going in for the kill. "Yes, and by Kallistos law, as your *wife*, what's yours is mine, baby." I'd probably regret my taunts, but I felt a rush when his nostrils flared. *Must have hit a nerve.* Without a second thought, I stepped forward and pressed my palm against his cheek. "So, this is our home now—especially if it's to become my new prison."

I brushed past him, needing to be anywhere but here before my adrenaline dissipated. I'd only taken two steps when he grasped my arm and pulled me into his body. Suddenly, we were nose to nose, every thought eddying from my mind. The comforting aroma of my coffee was dominated by the well-worn leather of his cologne and sharp remnants of his toothpaste as he crowded my space.

"This is not your prison," he said, gaze dropping to

my parted lips. "You are free to come and go as you please. And if you are already so eager to go back to your father, where the whole city knows you are abused, all you need to do is say the word. I can dissolve our marriage right now. By evening, you could be back in your childhood bedroom, locking your door and praying your father does not take his drunken anger out on you while you enjoy what is left of your life before the blood moon."

I couldn't breathe as his cruel yet true words sunk in. My body betrayed me as Rion's nose brushed my own. Whatever this was between us needed to stop. I warred with infatuation and infuriation, unsure of which to act upon or what I truly felt. Did I want to pull him closer? Or push him away before he could play with my heart?

"What will it be, Calia?"

"I don't want to die." It was the closest sentiment I could utter out loud without making myself sick, because I didn't want to say what I truly felt.

I want to stay with you.

His grip loosened around my bicep, as if the contact with my skin had burned him. I reached for the counter to stop myself from stumbling backward. He was so hot and cold; I couldn't get a reading on who he was or why he did the things he did. But I knew one thing.

I wanted to find out.

ten

Rion moved back to the table and began picking at the plate of food before him. "Take a seat," he said, wiping the corner of his mouth. "We have much to discuss."

He was the picture of nonchalance, acting as though nothing had happened between us. My erratically beating heart was proof otherwise. "I was going to make something for breakfast." I pointed at the fridge where I'd seen freshly cut fruit earlier.

"That is what I have staff for. Come and sit."

Before I could answer, a small man scurried into the kitchen. He began ushering me to the table, where my mug of coffee suddenly sat next to a glass of what looked like freshly squeezed orange juice. "What would you like to eat this morning?" he asked, averting his eyes so we never met.

"Um, fresh fruit, please." Rion grumbled something

about needing protein from the other side of the table. "And some eggs would be great, thank you."

The man dipped his head and began flitting around the kitchen at such a high speed he practically became a blur. Before long, he placed my breakfast before me, and my mouth watered. The scent of fresh herbs and butter from the eggs filled the air, and I groaned as I took my first bite. "Shit, this is good," I said, covering my mouth. The man smiled shyly before dipping his head again and running out of the room, the breeze comically fluttering a loose strand of my hair as he passed by.

Rion's scrutinizing gaze scanned me from head to toe, the unwelcome sensation causing a blush to creep along my already heated cheeks. I had no way of knowing what he was thinking, but I was sure I wasn't the type of woman that came to mind when he pictured his wife. I'd seen the tabloids, the women draped on his arm at public events. I glanced down at my thick thighs, shifting slightly in my seat.

Across the table, his hand tightened into a fist, causing me to shrink back. Whatever he saw in me, I was sure it was disappointing.

"What did you want to talk about?" I asked, breaking the awkward silence between us.

Rion leaned back in his chair, draping an arm across the one beside him. "As I stated last night, our marriage will be different than you might have expected."

"Yes, you made that clear," I said, staring down at the food on my plate.

He ignored my comment, pushing forward as if I'd

never said anything. "I will not ask you to adhere to anything I will not ask of myself. I do not care what relationships or entanglements you seek if they are not made public. We must *always* maintain a flawless image, or the tenuous peace our families have painstakingly curated will crumble in moments. Maintaining this is critical, Calia. Do you understand that?"

My fists ached, and I wanted to clench them and relieve the tension, but I didn't want him to know just how much his indifference bothered me. It was a feeling I was all too used to, and most of the time, I could shrug it off. But somehow, this was different. His aversion to being with me was starting to crack my strong façade.

I'd spent years building back my confidence after watching it be torn apart by people who didn't understand the consequences of their actions. From an early age, I was forced to realize how cruel the words of others could be and the damage they could inflictt. Most mornings, I dreaded waking up to don my school uniform, loathing the way classmates would snicker behind my back at the dimples along the back of my legs. Or how they would point out how different I looked from the others with my flaming locks. Money and status didn't matter. If anything, in my case, it made the situation worse.

But the whispering became unbearably loud in my mind, a constant loop of insults which began in their voices, but ended in my own.

The fact Rion was already unraveling the confidence I'd worked so hard for when I'd spent less than twenty-four hours with him was a low blow. I *should* be stronger. I *should* let his words roll off my back and pay him no mind. If he didn't like me, then that was his problem. Not mine.

But the word '*should*' was where dreams went to die. It was a dangerous complication that prevented me from standing up to the worst voice living freely in my mind.

Which was why I forced myself to keep my mouth shut—for fear of spilling out each dark insecurity plaguing me. Silently, I nodded.

Apparently, that wasn't good enough for my husband. "Use your words, Calia."

"Yes," I said, clearing my throat and averting my gaze. "I understand."

He watched me, waiting for any hint of a lie to cross my features. I should've spoken up and told him what I thought of his treatment. If we had any hope of making this work or being cordial, we had to be honest with each other. But I couldn't bring myself to hear his rejection. It was painful enough to have the thoughts racing through my mind; I didn't need to hear them confirmed aloud.

"This is not about you," he said quietly, peering down at the table where his fingers drew circles along the woodgrain. "You are a beautiful woman, Calia. Absolutely breathtaking, if I'm honest. However, you and I are not the same. We would not be compatible in any capacity other than acquaintances—friends at best —but never lovers."

It was like he reached into my mind and plucked my

thoughts from where I'd hidden them, and I hated it with every fiber of my being. His compliments didn't soften the blow, as I was sure he thought they would. Because my mind twisted his words into something they weren't.

"Of course," I said, offering him a brittle smile to attempt to mask the hurt as I sipped my now-cold coffee. The food on my plate was suddenly unappealing, and I pushed it away as I had so many times before when the sting of rejection washed over me.

His brows furrowed, looking between me and the plate. "Is there something wrong with your meal?"

"No, of course not. I'm just not hungry anymore." I forced a laugh, feeling it rattle against the hollow pit in my chest. "I guess my eyes were bigger than my stomach."

Rion didn't look convinced, but he didn't push the subject. "Our first appearance is minor, but it will be a test all the same—a way to see if we can pull off this ruse. At the end of the month, the mayor is holding a small charity gala at his penthouse. An invitation has been extended to us, given the excitement around our nuptials. My uncle will be there, as well as your father, so we cannot afford to slip up."

My back straightened at the mention of my father. If he was going to be there, perhaps my aunt would be, too. "Do you know if any of my other family will be in attendance?"

"I do not." I raised my brows, waiting to see if he would offer to find out, but nothing came "You will need to look your best. I have already arranged an appointment for you to be fitted for something proper."

"What's wrong with the outfits your mother picked out? Or any of the gowns hanging in my closet?" It was filled to the brim with clothing I never would wear. At least, not if I could help it. The wardrobe was devoid of color, filled with whites and creams, a disaster waiting to happen. I could hardly get through a day without spilling something on myself.

Rion shrugged, a piece of hair falling into his eyes. "Is there anything in there that interests you?"

"Well, no, but—"

"Then do not question my generosity. Just say thank you."

My already thinning patience was fraying further with each second I spent in his company. It was clear he had no tact when it came to speaking to another person. Which was fine as long as he didn't expect me to give him grace when he offered none in return. "You're exceedingly arrogant. Has anyone ever told you that before?"

"Many times."

"And?"

"And I do not care what others think of my conversational skills. I ensure my family, friends, and people have what they need. *That* is what I care about. And you, being my wife, will never want for anything again while you are with me."

"Except for pleasant conversation, perhaps."

He cocked his head to the side. "That is what you have Jasper for, is it not?"

I leaned forward, smiling as I braced my elbows on the table. It was a dangerous line to toe, and I'd probably regret my words somehow, but I never cared much about my safety. "Does that anger you?"

He matched my posture until we were mere inches away from one another. "This is the last thing I wanted to discuss. While I said I did not care what or who you did in your free time, Jasper is off-limits. Not only is he a staff member, but he is also my closest friend."

"So, you *are* angry," I murmured, pushing back. "Or is it jealousy? They both seem to have the same shade on you."

"*Neither,*" he growled, revealing a hint of the sharp canines underneath his lips. "But I will not tolerate you fucking the staff just because Jasper has given you some attention and you feel insecure. Allow me to let you in on a secret, wife; he does that with every woman who crosses his path. You are not special. He will fuck you, then leave you, and you will come crying to me with a broken heart because you assumed he cared. I simply do not want to deal with the fallout."

Rion sat back in his chair, stone-faced and resolute, but I had reached my limit. My eyes prickled with tears threatening to fall, and I refused to give him the satisfaction of knowing how deeply his words cut. I stood quickly, placing as much space between the two of us as I could without knocking my chair to the floor. His words rang out on repeat until it was all I could hear.

You are not special.
You are not special.
You are not special.

"This conversation is over," I said, attempting to keep my voice even. Gods, I was stupid. This man and I would never be on good terms. I was an inconvenience to his life, an irritating fly that he couldn't afford to squish. He didn't want this marriage any more than I did. The difference, however, was that I had been determined to make the most out of the shitty hand I'd been dealt, and he was not.

We were fundamentally different on every level, and he would never change. That much was abundantly clear.

His strong hand gripped my forearm, pulling me back into his hard body. "Where do you think you are going?"

"Anywhere you aren't." I pushed at his chest, but his hold only tightened. It bordered on painful, and I couldn't help but let out a small whimper which immediately had him releasing his grip. Red marks began forming where his fingertips had been, leaving behind a reminder of his disdain.

Something strange flickered in his eyes as he stared at the place he'd held. He ran a hand through his hair, tousling it in a stupid, unfortunate way that made him even more attractive before stepping back and straightening his posture. "I will find someone else to give you the grounds tour. I have work to do."

BRIELLE

How was your first night together? Did he bite you? Vampyres are known for their... talents in the bedroom. IS IT TRUE?

HEY! JUST CHECKING IN. I HAVEN'T HEARD FROM YOU THIS morning.

ARE YOU OKAY???

WHY ARE YOU IGNORING MY TEXTS???

I KNOW THAT HUSBAND OF YOURS HAS MORE enchantments on his home than the mayor, but I will break through them all to know you're okay! TEXT ME BACK!

I pinched the bridge of my nose as I stared down at Brielle's messages. She'd been sending a constant stream of questions since I woke up, but I wasn't in the mood to discuss my nigh. I mean, for fucks sake, what could I say? "Hey, Brielle! Sorry, I lost track of time talking to my husband who wants nothing to do with me. Oh, and I might have a crush on his super-hot friend and bodyguard? He made me hot cocoa last night when I couldn't sleep. Don't worry though—Rion told me it was nothing, and that I wasn't special. *kiss emoji*"

Yeah, that would calm her.

But I knew if I didn't give her something, she'd hold to her promise to storm this isle and fight past the wards to check on me. That was just what we did for one another; we cared. The most frustrating aspect of all this was that I didn't think I truly felt anything for Jasper other than friendship. I just wanted a friend. Someone I could turn to who knew this place like the back of his hand.

It wasn't my fault that my new friend was hot as sin.

My phone rang the next second—Brielle's name and photo lighting up on my screen. "Shit," I mumbled. I couldn't ignore her, not after the amount of texts she'd just sent.

"What's wrong?" she demanded before I could even get in a greeting. "And before you give me some bullshit about being tired or whatever, remember I will find out the truth, so you might as well save us both the trouble and spit it out."

I sighed, eyes drifting toward the picture of my mother sitting on my nightstand. She looked so beautiful and happy, eyes alight with laughter as she held me tightly. "It's just a lot to get used to. I mean, I knew what I was getting involved in. I knew our marriage would be fake and wasn't what I wanted for my life, but it's what I've got. Honestly, I'm just trying to make the most of it. But he is making it so godsdamn difficult, and I–"

"*Fake* marriage?" Somehow, I knew those were the two words she'd latch onto.

"Yeah, fake marriage. You know, the kind where you live in separate bedrooms and only speak to each other when necessary." Suddenly, I found myself spilling everything to her—even the bits I hadn't intended to disclose: Rion's proposal for extramarital relationships, the kitchen fiasco, and finally, how my new husband ended today's encounter. I even told her about the mundane tour of the estate I'd gone on with one of the household staff.

When I was done, and tears threatened to fall, she let out a breath. "Oh, Calia..." Pity filled her voice, and I hated the way it sounded.

"No, don't do that," I snapped, wiping away the single bead of moisture. "I'm fine. I'll be fine. I just need to get used to my new normal. It could be worse, right? He could have told me that if he couldn't have me, no one could. At least I have the freedom to do what I want."

"Do you, though?"

I fumbled with the ring on my finger; an ostentatious thing with a diamond big enough to be seen from the other side of Kallistos. I hated it with every fiber of my being, but it didn't surprise me that the D'Arcy family curated a piece of jewelry to so obviously showcase their wealth. "Of course I do. He said—"

"And yet, he also said that you can't pursue anything

with Jasper. Doesn't seem like complete freedom to me." When I said nothing, Brielle sighed, frustration building in her tone. "Calia, there has to be a way—"

I panicked, not wanting to talk about it anymore. Every time I did, I felt the same pang in my chest as I had with his rejection. "It's not that deep, Bri. I feel so much better after talking to you, okay? And listen, I don't know when, but Rion is funding a shopping spree. I need a fancy dress for the mayor's charity at the end of the month. Wanna join?"

At the change of topic, Brielle perked up and began talking enthusiastically about what I should wear. Brielle would be coming too, representing her family. Thankfully her mother had said she'd rather eat slugs than listen to the mayor drone on about his newest piece of real estate. At least I'd have one friendly face at my side.

eleven

Brielle and I ended our call with a promise on my end to let her know when the appointment was. I tossed the phone onto the sofa beside me, leaning back against the cushions. Silence descended, only the sound of my steady breathing kept me company.

During the tour, I'd lingered outside the library. The D'Arcy family had been around for centuries; I could only imagine the amount of books they owned. I didn't even care that they'd likely be about stuffy things like politics and *How to be a Dick 101*.

During college, I'd devoured classic literature, especially stories with grand, epic romances. While they'd always hold a special place in my heart, I quickly found that my tastes ran a bit naughtier. I'd once lost myself in a series about a woman blessed by the stars, sworn to one brother only to be destined for another. It was passionate and demanded your attention from the first page. However, the chances of me finding any books like *that* in the D'Arcy's private collection were slim.

But it was worth a shot.

Anything would be better than mindlessly scrolling on my phone, which I'd done for at least an hour before talking to Brielle. The amount of gossip already spreading about my marriage to Rion was insane. It ranged from a secret baby—*no, thank you*—to a love match—*not likely.*

Our picture was plastered across the front page of every newspaper, undoubtedly taken by Leonora, who'd snapped multiple shots as soon as we'd said 'I do.' At least whoever printed them took the time to digitally remove the bloodstains coating my white dress, because that was one reminder I didn't want.

With a groan, I pushed myself off the couch and walked into the hallway. I couldn't remember which direction led to the library, but it shouldn't be hard to find. It was somewhere on this floor, near the staircase I was warned away from.

That was yet another thing that piqued my interest, and with everyone otherwise occupied, this might be the best opportunity to find out what he was hiding up there.

"Fuck it," I muttered, walking toward what was sure to be a terrible idea. I couldn't fight the feeling there was something important no one was telling me. It didn't matter how often I tried to convince myself the secrecy was only Rion wanting his privacy; that slight tugging feeling lingered in my stomach and refused to dissipate.

All I had to do was go undetected by a houseful of vampyres with remarkable hearing, and make sure they didn't find out about my little escapade to snoop around Rion's stuff I had been explicitly forbidden from exploring.

Pfft. Yeah right.

Even if I managed to sneak by the rest of the household staff, Rion would know. I couldn't explain how I knew, but it was tied to that feeling tugging at my gut. I could almost picture the look on his face as my scent drifted to him in passing, indignation driving him to seek me out.

It didn't stop me. The heady thrill of wondering what he'd do if I was caught made my panties wetter than they had any right to be.

I quickly made my way to the winding stairway, taking care to step as lightly as possible on the well-worn wooden steps. As hard as it was, I tried not to use the handrail, worried it'd strengthen my scent. It didn't take long for me to reach the landing, and I was surprised to find it strangely homey. The dark walls matched those throughout the rest of the house, but the small corridor was littered with personal touches.

Pictures hung along the walls, dating back to gods only knew when. Some looked like antique tintypes, the images printed on thin metal—worn and faded in spots where fingers had touched over the years. I couldn't ignore my curiosity, allowing myself to linger and examine each one for as long as possible.

Raised voices sounded from down the hall, and my head snapped toward the door in fear. *Shit, shit, shit.* I was readying to bolt down the steps when I heard Leonora's voice. ". . .woo the girl, Rion. Make her love you, make her *trust* you. That is all I have asked."

"And you have asked for the impossible," he responded with a small snort.

"By the gods, Rion, are you truly so dense? She is the key to *everything*; without her, we have nothing. You must give her a reason to stay."

"Why?" he shot back. "She cannot go anywhere. And even if she tried, she would not last past the blood moon."

Leonora laughed, and the horrible feeling from earlier sunk to the bottom of my stomach. "And if she tries to run? Would you confine her to a cell to keep her here until we can do what we must? She might be safer that way, even now... I cannot lie and say I do not wonder what her blood might taste like. She smells delicious—"

The sharp sound of a hand striking a thick surface caused me to jump back. A floorboard creaked, and I realized I only had seconds to act. Less than, really. The voices went silent as I made my decision. Turning on my heel, I raced as quickly as I could down the stairway.

The only problem was I was nowhere near a match for my vampyre husband.

Rion's fingers dug into the soft flesh of my arm as he

slammed me into the wall. My head cracked against the hardwood, and I winced, tears filling my eyes as pain radiated down my neck and spine. My vision blurred, but I still saw how his lip curled, turning into an angry snarl.

"What the *fuck* were you doing, Calia? Spying on me?"

"N—No, I wasn't spying. I was just—"

"How much did you hear?" His breath fanned against my face, and I turned away, refusing to meet his gaze. His other hand snaked up and gripped my chin, jerking it back to him. "Do not look away, and do not deny it. *What. Did. You. Hear?*"

Each word was sharply punctuated, an accusation on his tongue to scare me into compliance. In that moment, he didn't see me as his wife. He saw an outsider who had thrust herself into his life in the most permanent way, a stain on his legacy and the key to his damnation.

Maybe part of that scared him. To know that if I decided I didn't want this anymore, I could walk right now and enjoy my last two and a half months of life without regret. I wasn't afraid to die—the end was inevitable—but I *was* afraid of not living. Of being so restrained by one person, place, or obligation that I forgot how beautiful life could be when you simply let go. Did he share the same opinion? Or did he prefer to lie to himself, pretending the life he was living was one he wanted?

"Answer me!" he roared, and I lost my self-control.

The tears I'd been trying to hold back came cascading down my face like a river that couldn't be stopped.

"Fuck. You. Let me go!"

He leaned closer, inhaling deeply as he caged me in like a wild animal. Something changed in his expression, his sensual lips parting and nostrils flaring. Carnal lust stared down at me, nearly stealing what little breath I had left.

The corner of his lips kicked up, the first sign of amusement I'd seen, even if it was edging on the side of cruel. "Are you scared of me, love?" His tongue darted out and brushed my neck, licking away the fallen wetness. "Your fear has a very distinct smell." I could feel the presence of his lips, the way he fought to keep them away from my pulse point. As though he could imagine how my blood would feel flowing freely into his mouth. "It would not hurt..."

He'd been right; I was scared. I was terrified, but not for the reasons he thought. I hated the possibility of dying without knowing what it felt like for him to possess my body. It would ruin me forevermore, decimating my body, mind, and soul until no other could come close. More so, I hated the way all of this made me feel. How could he hurt me, yell at me, piss me off more than anyone else, and still cause an ache between my legs unlike anything I'd ever felt? It wasn't natural, this attraction. In fact, it was dangerous.

Continuing down this path would have me eating out of the palm of his hand, so yes, I was terrified of what would become of me.

"Rion!"

I heard the voice clearly, yet all I could think of was the man holding my life between his calloused fingers. We stared at one another, unsure how to break the stalemate we constantly found ourselves in.

Suddenly, his body was yanked away from me, and I fell to the floor, gasping for breath. The heat of Rion's body faded away, and cold rushed in to take its place. The sudden rush of pain brought awareness to just how hard he'd been gripping me.

Jasper stood between Rion and me, releasing his hold on my husband's shoulder and pushing him backward. The buttons of Rion's navy shirt had been torn away, revealing more of that deep, jagged scar I'd seen the tip of earlier. Unimaginable brutality must have been used to leave a mark like that.

Jasper immediately helped me to my feet. His heavy hand ran along my jaw, neck, and shoulders to examine the damage done. The fluttering muscle in his jaw gave away just how bad it was. "Let's get you back to your room, yeah?"

"Wait," Rion called out, and I felt my heart stutter as it waited in stilted silence. He walked over and gripped my chin once more. "Do not ever spy on me again. Are we clear?"

This time, I refused to censor my speech, especially not for him. "Or *what*?" I hissed. "What'll you do, Rion?"

He tsked, tightening his grip. "Or I will truly give you a reason to fear me." He looked over my head and released his hold like I burned him. "Get her out of my sight."

My body tensed at the hurled threat, but my adrenaline dissipated into defeat as Jasper wrapped his arm around me. He tugged on me softly, prompting me to leave my husband behind, watching me walk away.

twelve

"Are you sure you are alright?" Jasper asked for what seemed like the hundredth time; I'd lost count after ten. After we returned to my room, he'd inspected me from head to toe, taking care as he examined around my neck where bruises were beginning to bloom along my skin.

Jasper sat a steaming mug of peppermint tea beside me, and I let the sweet mint wash over me. I'd always been drawn to the scent; it reminded me of my mother's favorite essential oil. She often used it in her baths, turning the room into a small sauna. It would seep through the top floor of the house, bringing with it a comfort I hadn't known since her death. Reaching over, I grabbed the drink and hugged it tightly. "I'll be fine, I promise."

It wasn't a complete lie; My body would be fine, even if I had a migraine, but I wouldn't be able to forget Rion's words. That was the first time he'd shown any emotion, and he'd flown into a blind rage when he thought I'd heard something I wasn't supposed to. Which begged the question: What were Leonora and Rion hiding?

My gaze drifted back toward Jasper, sitting on my couch with his head in his hands. It seemed as though he lingered there just in case I fell to pieces and needed help picking them up. But now that I was safe in my own space, I knew I wouldn't break further.

"Want to tell me what you were doing before he attacked you?"

I debated lying to him, but knew Rion would likely tell him the truth. Jasper was the closest thing I had to an ally here, and I couldn't risk jeopardizing that. "I, uh, got bored and wandered through the house. I was going to visit the library, but..." I trailed off, forcing myself to take a breath. Would he tell me I deserved it once he discovered what I'd done? It wasn't like I'd committed a murder, but I was curious about Rion. Not only who he is now, but who he was before—his interests, his dislikes, what makes him, well, *him*.

Jasper's eyes widened a bit, waiting for me to continue. "He'd told me his rooms were off limits, including the staircase leading up to that small tower. I let curiosity get the best of me. He was having a conversation with Leonora and—" I shrugged.

"Ah," he said, hanging his head slightly. "Rion's always been a strange one about his privacy. He had a rough childhood."

I snorted. "Yeah, real rough growing up with loving parents and unlimited wealth."

Jasper furrowed his brows. "Do not judge a man you do not know too harshly. His father? Yes, his father was an amazing man—one of the best."

"And his mother?" I asked..

Jasper huffed. "Leonora cares about one person and one person only. Herself. When Ramsey was away... Calia, she did horrible things to Rion. She pushed him to his limits repeatedly, testing his abilities and powers. There were days he could barely walk, yet she still forced him to train."

I brought the mug to my lips, thinking about the similarities between our families. "Why didn't he ever tell his father what happened when he was away?"

"He tried. Or at least, he tried *once*. His father confronted Leonora and demanded she explain herself. She'd made a mistake, you see. Normally, she'd back off a few days before Ramsey would return, but this time, he'd come back early. Rion's body was littered with bruises. When Leonora couldn't explain, he placed her in the deprivation chamber for two weeks."

I gaped. "The what?"

"It's like a cell, but you are completely disconnected from your senses. There's no light, no sound, no sustenance. It's fucking hell," he said, running a hand behind his neck.

"How would you know? Have you been in it?"

He gave me a cheeky grin. "Once. Rion and I were

just kids. We'd gotten the bright idea to play catch with one of his ancestors' urns."

I grimaced. "Oh, no."

"Oh, yes. As you can imagine, the coordination of two gangly ten year old boys was not the best. His father walked in right as the urn shattered against the floor. Ashes went everywhere—it was complete and total chaos. That's one of the few times I'd ever seen his father lose his temper. He went completely red in the face and started screaming at us. Then, he forced us to clean up the ashes and place them in a new urn before he took us down to the chamber. We spent one hour in there, which was the most terrifying hour of my life."

We both laughed, and for the first time since I'd arrived, I felt some semblance of peace. It was nice having a friend who wouldn't hesitate to step in on my behalf. I fought a yawn, and he pushed to his feet.

"I'll let you rest. Do you need me to help you to the bed?" He held out his hand, and I wanted to take it, but I shook my head and laid it against the cushion. There was a perfect view of the lake from where I sat.

"No, I think I'll stay here a little longer, but thank you," I said, turning my head to gaze out. The crescent moon glittered, the first hints of red beginning to peek through.

I'd never seen the fabled blood moon. It was an phenomenon that occurred once every century. But I'd heard my aunt and uncle discuss it—how tensions were higher between the fae and the vampyres around that time. She always looked fearful whenever it was mentioned, quickly shutting down and taking me out of the room before I could learn more.

But it drew closer, and I felt a strange current lingering under my skin. A restlessness I couldn't shake. However, I could also attribute that to my asshole of a husband.

Jasper said his goodbyes, slipping out the door and leaving me to my thoughts. I didn't want to think about Rion anymore; he'd occupied more than enough of my time. Instead, I reached for a book on the small table beside me and lost myself in the story.

A LOUD THUMP SOUNDED OUTSIDE MY DOOR, JERKING ME from a restless sleep. I looked around the room with bleary eyes, shielding them from the light shining down from the reading lamp. I'd stayed up way later than I intended to, giving up on the world of polite societies I'd immersed myself in to instead pull up my favorite steamy read on my phone. One smutty scene led to another, and I'd forced myself to keep my eyes open until I apparently lost the battle.

A string of curses met my ears, followed by a low grunt of pain. "... fucking idiot," they said. "Stupid, fucking idiot."

I stood up and walked toward the door. "Hello? Who's there?"

There was a huff, followed by a long pause. "Nobody you would care to see."

"Rion?" His name was out of my mouth before I could stop it, which had me closing my eyes and mentally berating myself for showing my cards like this. And it wasn't that I hated him—I didn't know him enough to make that judgment. But I sure as hell didn't like him, not after how he'd been today.

We were as different as two people could be.

"Ah, I knew you would figure it out."

I fought a smile. "Well, you *are* an arrogant ass." There was another loud thump, and I pictured him letting his head fall back against the wood. "Anyway, what're you doing here? It's late."

"Yes, thank you for that observation, *wife*. I had not noticed." His words faltered as a small hiccup escaped him. "I have been told, very insistently, I might add, that I need to apologize to you. But can I confess? Apologies are not my strong suit, love."

"Is that right?"

"Yup." He ended the word with an exaggerated pop. "It may shock you, but I do not often find myself in positions where I have to do this sort of thing. Or even feel the need to. I have never had to answer to someone like you."

I couldn't help but chuckle, wondering what he was doing on the other side of this barrier between us. "What?" I gasped in fake shock. "You could've fooled me."

I slid down the door, placing my back against the

wood. This was a peek at yet another avenue of what made Rion D'Arcy the enigmatic alphahole he was. And like an eager explorer, I wanted to traverse each of those paths and study him. What made him tick? What pushed him to get out of bed in the morning? Who and what did he love with his whole being? What quality would enable someone to slip past his walls?

Would I be okay never possessing it?

Because I was right; there was more to this man than met the eye. I could only imagine the number of people he allowed to see him like this was minute, and now I was among their company. Frankly, the drastic change in disposition gave me whiplash. Still, I selfishly wanted to know everything about him.

"You know, you are not innocent in this either," he sighed. "I do not feel like I asked much of you, Calia. I asked you to respect my privacy. You snooped where I told you not to snoop. You forced my hand—"

I cut him off before he could say anything further. "Nuh-uh. You don't get to do that. You don't get to turn this around on me because you have no self-control regarding your anger." I ran my fingers through my tangled hair before letting them fall onto my lap. "I just want to know more about the man I married, Rion. Is that so bad?"

He was silent for a long moment. So long, I'd thought he'd fallen asleep or left. "Yes. It is," he whispered. The door muffled his words, but I felt them all the same.

"And why is that?"

Rion blew out a breath. "Which excuse would you like me to use, Calia? That I am not a good man? That I am incapable of love or affection? Or I could give you my personal favorite, that I will lead to your ruination. Take your pick because all are true."

My hands gripped the underside of my thighs, picking at my skin as our conversation drifted into dangerous territory. "I don't think that's true."

He scoffed. "Then you are a bigger idiot than I took you for, love."

"Hey! Aren't you supposed to be apologizing? You're doing a shit job so far."

He laughed, a real one, and my stupid little heart flipped. It was traitorous, and I hated how I wanted to hear it again. "That's right, that's right." Rion cleared his throat before groaning. "I should have taken Jasper up on his offer to write down what I should say. To be fair, he also told me not to get drunk—or rather, any more than I was—but here I am."

"I'd rather hear what you have to say, anyway. I don't want to hear Jasper's words; I want yours."

"You will regret that when I can come up with nothing better than 'I'm sorry,'" he mumbled. "Because that is all I have, Calia. And I do not even know if I am truly sorry for what happened, other than my poor reac-tion. I should not have—" His voice grew tight before he stopped and blew a sharp breath. My chest ached knowing how difficult this was to him, hearing the apology he truly wanted to give in the way he spoke. "I should never have put my hands on you. I was serious when I told you I was a private man, and that will not ever change, but I should never have taken my anger out on you. And for that, I truly am sorry because you deserve so much more."

I let everything he said sink in, warring between frustration that we were in this situation and exhilaration because this was a side I never thought I'd see. And for once, I didn't question his motives or truth, because I could hear it in his voice. Men like Rion D'Arcy didn't apologize. He'd admitted that much himself.

And yet, he did for you...

But why? Was it the lowered inhibitions driven by alcohol-infused guilt? Or had his guilt driven him to drink?

"I knew I should not have come here. It was foolish to hope that you would accept my apology." I was on my feet before he could heave himself off the ground, yanking open the door and reaching for his hand.

"I accept your apology," I said breathlessly, stopping him from walking away.

Rion stared down at me with wild eyes, his nostrils widening as he scanned down my body. His shirt was untucked and ruffled. The top buttons were undone, displaying the slightest smattering of hair across his pecs. I could make out the faint outline of his scar running deep through his skin, and I fought my desire to trace the old injury with my fingers. The sharp tang of alcohol clung to his skin, filling the space between us with the evidence of how much liquid courage he'd needed to show up at my door.

He stepped toward me, his hand lingering in mine until we were chest to chest. I tilted my head to get a better look at him. He leaned in, teasing me with his slow approach as I licked my lips, drawing attention to my mouth. His hand came up, tilting my chin further until my neck was fully elongated.

"What're you doing?" I whispered. Every thought eddied from my mind, and all I could focus on was the intense heat burning in his gaze and the tender ache between my thighs. He was powerful, strong, brash, and rude, but something tender lived inside, begging to be freed.

He leaned in further until I felt his breath fan out across my face. "I do not know," he confessed. "But I want to find out."

With a thundering heart, his lips touched mine, and I exploded with need. I was on fire, and the only thing that could save me was this kiss—this *man*. And if it didn't, I would gladly allow my soul to smolder as I burned for him. It was nothing and everything all at once.

My hands slid around his neck, pulling his body even closer to mine. His palm landed on my lower back, traveling down to my ass and gripping it tightly. Rion groaned into my mouth as he slid his fingertips beneath the silk fabric.

"Fuck, Calia. This is not...we should not..."

But his feeble protests didn't correlate with the frantic way he tugged me closer. He lifted me and I wrapped my legs around his waist, feeling the inescapable sign of his arousal. *Fuck.* He was impossibly hard and thick. A thousand filthy scenarios flitted through my mind, each one dirtier than the last. I ground against him, seeking friction and feeling powerful as he gripped me tighter each time I did so.

"I want you," I said, leaning my head back as he pressed open-mouthed kisses along my neck. "Please, Rion... I—"

Suddenly, he dropped me to the floor and stepped away. His chest was heaving, and I didn't know what had triggered his flight response until I felt the cool rush of air against the spots he'd just been laving with his tongue. My hair had fallen back, exposing the bruises along my collarbone where his hands had been hours before.

His silver eyes bled to near white with rage, fists clenched at his side. "You were so eager to be ravished that you'd forgotten about the marks I put on you in anger?" he laughed darkly, shaking his head.

I blinked back tears, feeling a mix of emotions. He was right; I had forgotten about the marks, but it wasn't because I wanted his dick. It was because I wanted *him*. Or maybe I just wanted to be wanted *by* him. And then shame set in because this was how he chose to reject me —by mocking me.

Yet again, I was left reeling from his hot-to-cold act, cursing myself for thinking I was gaining any traction. *What the hell is wrong with you, Calia?*

He pointed at my neck, the veins in his arms straining against his skin. "That is exactly why I am no good for you. You are breakable, Calia, in more ways than one. One day, I *will* destroy you, and you will be powerless to stop me. Mark my fucking words."

"You're pathetic," I said, shaking my head. The words slipped out quickly, and at that point, I didn't want to stop. I wanted to tell him how unbelievably stupid he was being and give him an ounce of the mistreatment he'd given back. "You won't let anyone in to see the real you because you're too scared to handle their judgment if they don't like what they see. And that, Rion, would *destroy* you, wouldn't it?"

We stared at one another for an eternity, and I resisted the voice telling me to apologize—to smooth things over. What was I sorry about? For speaking my mind when I normally censored my thoughts? No, tonight was supposed to be about his apologies. Not mine.

He dipped his chin before raising to his full height and straightening his shoulders. The fervent man I'd spent the past half hour with restored the cold-hearted façade I'd become so familiar with. Rion turned to walk away, but that didn't stop me from calling out to him again.

"There will come a time when *you* need something from *me*, and I'll be more than happy to watch you beg. Mark *my* words, husband."

thirteen

Over the following weeks, I created a semblance of a daily routine.

I'd wake up, dragging myself to the kitchen to make breakfast and coffee. I avoided Rion's mercurial gaze coming from the breakfast nook in the corner before slipping back up to my room and settling into the chair on my balcony to watch the sunrise.

Hating him took up too much time and energy, so if he wanted to carry on his life as though I wasn't here, I'd let him. I'd been serious when I told him the day would come when he would need something from me, and when it did, I'd be damned if I gave into his bedroom eyes and disarming charm.

After breakfast, I'd shower and get dressed before wandering down to the library—without any detours—and pick up a new book to lose myself in. I'd broadened my horizons since I'd realized the D'Arcy's collection lacked the more enjoyable varieties of literature, but that hadn't stopped me from occasionally asking Jasper to order some of my more scandalous favorites.

"Why won't you ask Rion to do this for you?" he'd questioned once as I handed him my second list of novels to source. My response came in the form of a deadpan look as he pocketed the piece of paper and laughed.

Later, I'd generally find myself walking along the banks of the Odesza. The D'Arcy's landscape was breathtaking—boasting green lawns, a small hedge maze, and dog kennels. There was an atrium-like building off the kitchens where I often saw Rion reading a book or watching the birds flutter through the trees underneath the sun.

Sometimes, the sight would steal the breath from my lungs, especially as he tipped his head to the sky and closed his eyes. In that singular moment, even if he didn't know it, he allowed me to see him without the walls he'd constructed around him. Too often, I took the sun's warmth for granted, especially as I longed to feel the kiss of the moon's cold breath. But I couldn't let him occupy more of my thoughts than he already did, so I focused on the dogs.

They quickly became my favorite thing about being a D'Arcy. I quickly befriended their caretaker, enjoying her company and the reprieve she brought.

In the evenings, Leonora forced the family to sit together for dinner. She and Renwick sat on one side of the table while Rion and I sat on the other. They carried on the conversation well enough without my input, only occasionally directing it to me. The topics lacked any real substance. Leonora often filled any awkward silence by prattling on about who she had lunch with that day or how much she spent at the stores where she shopped.

Renwick, I'd noticed, was a keen observer. He and Rion were similar in that regard, but something in his uncle's gaze made me uncomfortable. Sometimes, when he stared at me, it felt like he was taking a knife and peeling back that first layer of skin. But I couldn't figure out what he was searching for. I thought myself an open book, never hiding my emotions, but rather, keeping them under control. So, what was there to find that I didn't already give freely?

Jasper often walked me back to my room after dinner. Sometimes we'd make idle conversation, but others; we just enjoyed the companionable silence. Each time, I'd feel Rion's stare on my back with every step I took from him, but he never intervened.

He always let me walk away.

Once I was safely tucked away on my couch for the evening, I couldn't miss the unmistakable squeal of tires as Rion's car tore out of the driveway and into the night. I never knew where he went, nor did I ask. Honestly, I didn't think I even wanted to know.

There'd been a woman I'd seen come by the house on occasion, making her way to Rion's office without so much as a hello. No one stopped her. If anything, they greeted her with a kindness I'd never received. Even

Jasper wouldn't tell me anything about her, claiming it wasn't his place.

"If Rion wanted to make her presence known to you, he would, Calia. I can't get involved."

Rion owed me nothing, not anymore. I was done pretending we could be something we weren't. My new reality was quiet, but there was comfort in knowing I also didn't owe any explanations to anyone. I was left to my own devices, and after a lifetime of living under my father's rule, it was nice to have a quiet sense of freedom.

Brielle had come over several times, typically staying a night or two over the weekend. Rion conveniently had business that required him to stay in the city when she was over, taking Jasper along. We were aggressively surveilled by Atlas, who took his job far too seriously. We were afforded no privacy without him being more than a few feet away. As it was, he was permanently stationed outside my door until Jasper and Rion returned.

The time had come for my dress fitting appointment in preparation for the mayor's gala. Brielle had shown up early in the morning, bringing a gift from my favorite bakery on the other side of town—a dark chocolate croissant and a scalding hot cappuccino.

"Gods, you're a lifesaver," I said by way of greeting, taking the cup from her outstretched hand and inhaling the bitter aroma.

"Yes, good morning to you too, Cal! I'm great, by the way. Thanks for asking," she said with a smile and a roll of her eyes before pulling me in for a hug.

"Careful! I don't want to squish the croissant," I muttered, holding it away from our bodies.

She swatted my arm before taking a sip of her coffee. "Who's our bodyguard this morning?" she asked, looking over my shoulder to where Atlas shifted on his feet at the bottom of the staircase.

"That'd be me," Jasper called, stepping out of the hallway in a crisp grey suit. The top two buttons were undone, and Brielle's jaw dropped as she took him in.

I pinched her side. "You're drooling," I whispered in her ear.

"And you aren't?"

Jasper smiled, sliding his hands into his pockets. "You both are. If you're quite finished objectifying me, I believe we have an appointment to make."

I opened my mouth to object, but the twinkle in his eye told me not to bother. We'd been caught red-handed. "Yeah, Brielle. Stop ogling my staff," I muttered, fighting a laugh as she turned to me in shock.

"You little shit," she whispered, pushing me toward the car waiting in the garage.

Brielle lounged along the chaise, a glass of champagne in her hand as she eyed my dress with envy. A large chandelier sparkled above us, the light reflecting off the crystals onto the dark navy walls of the fitting room.

"Damn, girl!" she said, whistling low. "You look amazing. Turn around!"

I looked down, doing a small twirl for my cousin. The emerald velvet was soft beneath my fingers, highlighting my neckline and chest as it draped over one shoulder. The a-line gown highlighted my waist before flowing gracefully over my wide hips, the hem pooling along the floor. I wasn't sure I'd ever been in something so luxurious. It was simple. Timeless. And for once, I felt stunning, loving the shape of my body rather than resenting it.

I was absolutely in love with the way it made me feel. Brielle's smile was contagious, and it didn't take long before we were giggling like schoolgirls.

The designer quickly ushered me back to the changing room so she could make the appropriate alterations and show Brielle the design she'd created for her. Rion had been gracious enough to ensure my cousin's wardrobe was also covered.

A present, he said, to act as a treaty between the two of us.

While I accepted the offering, the truth was that I'd only felt indifference toward my husband since that drunken night. The bruising around my neck had faded quickly, leaving my memories as the only reminder of what had happened. He'd been careful to avoid me at all costs, but that would change the night of the mayor's party.

I wasn't sure how we were supposed to act as though we were madly in love when we'd hardly spent time with one another. Could he play the part of a doting husband so easily? Could I be his adoring wife?

Rion didn't strike me as the type to show affection so easily, but even I was curious to see if we could pull our ruse off in a room full of people. Especially when they were ready to scrutinize every aspect of our relationship.

Once the designer had finished, I retreated to the main room and took Brielle's place on the chaise. I reached for my drink, watching the bubbles dance inside the crystal glass. It didn't take long for Brielle to strut down the small runway, showing off her figure in a gorgeous silver dress that shimmered like a thousand diamonds.

I held my hand up to shield my eyes. "You're liable to blind someone in that thing."

She twirled dramatically, squealing in delight at her reflection in the gilded mirror. "I know! Isn't it wonderful? Get up here!"

Brielle grabbed my arm and pulled me beside her, taking out her phone to snap pictures of us. We made funny faces, nearly collapsing with laughter. We'd both had a few drinks, and I let the stress of the past month fall from my shoulders. I deserved this. Hell, we both did. Brielle had been busting her ass at my aunt's charity for the past six months, working on funding for a home for children who were victims of household violence.

"Did you ever think our lives would end up like this?" I asked, resting my hand on hers as she wrapped it around my waist.

She snorted. "Nope. I thought we'd bust out of the

city when you turned eighteen and travel the world. We'd meet hot men—not boys—who'd spoil us rotten. When they got on our nerves, we'd move on to the next ones because," she gestured down her long body, "look at us."

A throat cleared behind us, and I glanced up. Jasper's golden eyes met mine through the mirror as he leaned on the doorframe. His gaze threatened to burn me alive, but I stayed rooted to my spot. We had toyed a fine line since the night in the kitchen. We were friends, nothing more, but there were moments I caught him watching me in a way that made me wonder what was on his mind...or mine.

Like the way he was right now.

I hated how it made me feel—not knowing if it was truly Jasper causing heat to radiate between my thighs, or if it was just because I'd gone so long without inti-mate contact. The only exception had been the drunken kiss with Rion, and I'd spent every night since then chasing a high I'd been unable to achieve. My fingers alone were incapable of quenching the constant ache.

"It's time to go," Jasper said, lowering his voice. I blushed furiously, hoping my thoughts weren't written across my face.

Brielle's giggle broke my trance, and we went through the curtain to return our dresses to the seam-stress and change back into our regular clothes. "Your gowns will be ready tomorrow morning," she said in a thick accent. Her wrinkled hands delicately placed a protective bag over them. "The designer is a very busy woman. Do not be late, or I will give them to someone else."

"You're not the designer?" I asked, raising a brow. I'd assumed, apparently incorrectly, that she'd been the one to create these beautiful gowns.

Her only response was a sharp shake of her head before disappearing to the back.

We stepped into the humid underground garage, immediately missing the air-conditioned building. "Shit," Brielle cursed, sifting through her bag. "I forgot my phone. It'll just take a second."

"Hurry up, Bri. It's hot as hell." I hated the heat and everything it brought with it. Sweat had begun to drip down my neck the moment we left the boutique.

She waved me off as Atlas followed her back into the shop, leaving Jasper and me alone. "Did you enjoy yourself?" he asked, eyes scanning the area as we made our way to the slick, black SUV parked at the end.

I nodded. "It was nice to get out of the house for a bit. I didn't think I'd miss the city like I did, but now that I'm here? I don't know. It's just nice to be back."

He said nothing, slipping his hand into his pocket and fishing out the electronic key to start the car. There was something sexy about it, but I quickly dismissed the thought. I shouldn't be thinking about how his clothing stretched against his muscles.

Brielle's voice sounded from behind us, and I placed my hand on Jasper's arm to stop him as we waited. "I'm going to start the car," he mumbled. "It's hot as fuck."

I barely registered the faint click of the remote as it

was swallowed by a boom that knocked me to the ground. Debris fell around us, peppering us with metal shards and broken glass. Someone pushed me out of the way, but not quickly enough. My head bounced off the concrete, darkening the edges of my vision as I fought to stay conscious.

fourteen

Don't close your eyes. Stay awake. Focus on your senses.

I stared ahead, watching as rampant flames consumed our SUV. Thick plumes of smoke rose into the air, the metal charred and melting away from the frame. We'd almost *died*. If Brielle hadn't gone back for her phone, our blood would have been splattered across the pavement.

Jasper lay just feet away, a large piece of metal protruding from his leg. He blinked rapidly. Gunshots sounded from behind other vehicles, mixing with the screams of passersby.

What the hell was happening?

"Cal!"

Brielle. She was here. She had been with me. But where?

I pushed off the ground, looking behind me. She

and Atlas were crouched behind a minivan, taking cover as rapid gunfire came from across the garage. Blood leaked from a wound at her temple, but she looked unharmed otherwise.

"Cal, get down!"

Three masked figures darted in our direction, each with large rifles strapped to their backs and pistols in their hands. Atlas fired shots in their direction, but he wasn't quick enough to dodge as one of the assailants fired.

It happened in slow motion. A bullet landed directly between Atlas's eyes, and his body fell to the ground with a heavy thud. His head shifted to the side, a dull, lifeless gaze staring blankly back at me. Brielle screamed in horror as blood pooled around his head, slowly spreading toward her feet.

"Jasper! Jasper, get up!" I bellowed, crawling over to where he lay. He looked unfocused, having taken the brunt of the explosion. A deep gash split the skin of his neck from below his ear to his sternum. Vampyres healed quickly, but it wasn't happening quickly enough, given his extensive injuries.

There was something I could do to help, but it was stupid. More than that, it was incredibly reckless. If I was wrong, it could kill me.

But I could die either way. I didn't know what would happen if the gunmen made it over to us. This would be my choice. Even if it had disastrous consequences, it might be enough to get Brielle out of harm.

I picked up a piece of glass and sliced my palm open.

Jasper's eyes widened, the first sign of focus I'd seen since the explosion. "Drink."

"No," he rasped, shaking his head in horror. "I cannot—"

"You have to." Each second he delayed brought us one step closer to a grim fate. The squeal of tires reached my ears as a matte black van skidded to a stop. Several figures filed out, their weapons drawn and trained on us. He watched them with caution before gripping my arm and yanking me forward.

The moment his lips touched my skin, excruciating pain radiated through my arm. The sensation was increasingly horrific with each pull he took of my blood. It was nothing like what I'd experienced with Rion during our wedding ceremony. His gaze grew hooded, the gold of his eyes disappearing until they became wholly black.

Brielle shouted my name repeatedly in warning, but I couldn't draw myself away from the havoc Jasper was wreaking on my body. Arms banded across my chest, yanking me away from Jasper's hold. The move tore my flesh, leaving a gaping wound where his mouth had been seconds prior.

"Got her," a gruff voice called, tossing me over his shoulder.

Shit, shit, shit! If they put me in their van, I was as good as dead. My uncle had drilled that into my head from an early age. "*If anyone takes you, little star, the chances of us finding you diminish.*"

I thrashed in his hold, maneuvering my body until I

could connect my knee with his nose. He cursed, tightening his grip across my ass. "She better be fuckin' worth this shit!"

My blood loss was becoming evident, causing the world to spin with each step the man took toward the van. We were only a few feet away, and my fight was dwindling. All I wanted to do was close my eyes and rest.

I met Brielle's terrified gaze. She pressed her phone to her ear and mumbled something into the speaker. "I love you," I mouthed, and she shook her head as tears slipped from her eyes.

If I was going to die, she would be the last person I'd see. Though I hated the thought of her having to witness me like this. Jasper was gone. Crimson stained the concrete where we'd been, a reminder of the choice I'd made that would likely cost me my life.

I'd never been afraid to die, not even when I was told about the death clause in my marriage contract. But this? This was terrifying.

The back doors of the van swung open, and my body slammed against the metal floorboard. My arms were roughly wrenched behind me and zip-tied together. "Careful! If we fuck her up much more, the boss'll have a fit."

"Let's hope she even makes it. That vamp took a bite outta her, and now she ain't lookin' so good."

"We gotta stop that bleeding." I felt someone turn my wrist to apply a bandage. "What're you sitting around for? Drive, you idiot!" The vehicle lurched forward, followed by the slamming of doors and squeal of tires.

The faraway sound of sirens zoomed past us as we fled the scene, leaving Brielle and Jasper behind. I rolled over, pressing my face into the cool floor just in time to throw up what little food I had in my stomach. Inexplicably, my attention fell on an errant screw, bouncing and skittering across the floor of the van. I thought it sounded like the tinkling of a bell as my vision faded, and I sunk into darkness

THE SOUND OF SCREAMED CURSES BROUGHT ME BACK TO consciousness just before the entire world turned upside down. We were falling down a steep hill, the van rolling roughly. My body was tossed around like a doll. Something sharp stabbed into my side, slicing me open. Hot, sticky blood coated my skin, pouring fresh from the new wound.

I'd been right. I was going to die.

We came to a halt, dust hanging in thick clouds around the vehicle. The copper tang of blood mingled with the acrid bite of fuel. No matter how often I tried to clear my vision, the world remained out of focus. Muted voices echoed in my head, the air filling with gunshots once again.

I was so tired. I just wanted to sleep. If I could close

my eyes, the pain would disappear, even if only for a moment.

Just one single moment.

The sound of metal shredding under sharp claws drew my attention to the back of the van. Thin streams of light filtered through gaping holes left behind from the destruction. ". . . have to get her out—it's gonna blow."

The doors were ripped open, and I saw a man, silhouetted against the bright light, his features obscured by shadow. I allowed myself to be taken by the darkness once more.

Maybe death wouldn't be so bad after all...

fifteen

"Fucking find them," a harsh voice gritted out. A steady yet incessantly annoying beep filled the silence between their words, making it hard to concentrate on what was happening. "I do not care what it takes. Make it happen."

My eyelids were heavy as I tried to lift them, and every part of my body ached. I groaned, unable to do more than twitch my fingers. "She's waking up," the voice said sharply.

My memories were foggy. I could easily recall the sound of gunfire and crumpling metal as we flipped down the hill rapidly, flashes of the overwhelming anxiety that accompanied the thought of dying, and the fear of being abandoned by Jasper, but nothing concrete.

I blinked, clearing my vision. An older man in a sharp white jacket strode through the door, a clipboard tucked under his arm. He walked over and checked something on a monitor near the bed before flashing a professional smile my way. "Ah, Calia. It's wonderful to see you awake!" He leaned forward conspiratorially. "You gave everyone quite a scare when they brought you in."

Did I? Other than Brielle, who I hoped had left the area unharmed, I wasn't sure who else would've been worried. And how long had I been out?

". . .Your aunt and uncle are just outside, along with your cousin, and Mr. D'Arcy here hasn't left your room even for a moment."

That was when I noticed someone sitting in the corner, their eyes dark and lips pinched. *Rion.* A muscle ticked in his jaw, his hands gripping the armrests of his chair. *He didn't care for being called out like that.* I didn't care for it either because I'd forgotten I was hooked up to a heart monitor that gave away the rush I felt at knowing Rion was *worried.* But why would he be worried? Was there more to this than he said? And would he have been free to live his life if I'd died in the accident, or would the death clause have still found a way to take him?

Erratic beeping filled the room, both men's attention turning to the machine. The sound only worsened as I looked over at my husband, and noticed a smug smirk plastered to his stupid, handsome face as he realized its indication.

The doctor chuckled and turned the monitor's volume down, thankfully not addressing it further. He ran through a list of injuries I'd sustained, stating he was surprised I was healing so quickly given how garish I looked when I arrived. "The only wound that will leave scarring is the one on your hand. I'm afraid the damage was extensive, given the venom injected into your system."

"Venom?" I echoed. "But I hadn't—" Visions of Jasper's teeth tearing into my skin raced back—the agony I felt with each drag, and how the wound had been torn as the men grabbed me. I raised my palm and stared at the abnormal lines.

"Thankfully, it shouldn't leave any lingering effects." The doctor glanced behind him at Rion, whose face grew red. "For what it's worth, it appears the... injection was an accident. Given the amount, an involuntary reaction likely occurred in a moment of a desperatation."

"It should not have fucking happened at all," Rion muttered bitterly, talking more to himself than the room.

"Yes, well, it did. We can be thankful a scar is the only evidence," the doctor said. He patted my shoulder and excused himself to tell my aunt and uncle I was awake, leaving Rion and me in stilted silence.

I didn't know what to say, especially not when his stormy eyes landed on me. "Why were you so reckless?" he asked.

I shrank back into the pillows. "What's that supposed to mean? We were ambushed, and I—"

"Why did you let him drink from you?" he exploded, leaning forward. He braced his arms on his knees. His usually polished appearance had vanished. The top of his shirt was unbuttoned, and his sleeves were rolled up to just below his elbow, showing off his forearms in a way that should have been illegal. However, amidst my ogling I noticed substantial burns darkening his skin and marring his tattoos. What had happened to him to create such damage?

"Do you realize what could have happened? You could have died!"

My thoughts evaporated as quickly as they had begun. "I could have died either way. I saw a possible way out, and I took it." I fiddled with the edge of my sheets, avoiding his penetrating gaze as long as possible.

I knew what I'd done was reckless. If I could go back, I wondered if it would play out the same way. Either way, I was damn sure I didn't need him yelling at me for the choices I couldn't change.

He scoffed. "Do not be so naïve. That is a fool's answer, and you do not strike me as a fool, Calia."

Prick. He hadn't been there. He hadn't known how terrified I was of meeting my demise or surviving in a world where Brielle no longer breathed. "I was trying to save Brielle. Jasper wasn't healing fast enough, and Atlas had just been shot. I saw no other way out. And what happened to your own skin? Where did *those* marks come from?"

"That is not—" His phone began ringing, and he stared at the screen only a moment before answering. "Yes?"

The sound of a soft female's voice came through,

causing whatever restraint I had to dissipate. Not only had he taken a call in the middle of our conversation, but he had made my place in his life *very* clear.

"I have already told you," he said, looking my way. "This weekend is not ideal. I will be in contact when I can accommodate you." He ended the call, opening his mouth to speak again, but I was done.

I'd heard enough. A migraine was pounding relentlessly in my head, and I was in no mood to be chastis—especially by him. I closed my eyes, taking in a deep breath before interrupting, "Why do you care, Rion?"

sixteen

The door swung open, and my family rushed to my side with panic-stricken faces before Rion or I could say anything. They fussed over me for ten minutes, asking the doctors about my recovery. I'd been unconscious for two days and would be kept overnight for further observation. If nothing went wrong, I'd be released in the morning. Rion hadn't moved from his seat in the corner, watching us all with careful eyes.

My aunt was talking so fast that I barely registered what she was saying. "I'll make sure to get all of your favorite foods when I order groceries, and I'll tell the staff to ready your room—"

"No."

Every head in the room turned in Rion's direction. "What do you mean 'no'?" my aunt asked, crossing her arms.

"She is my wife, so she will be cared for in *our* home. Not yours."

My aunt opened her mouth to argue, but I leaned forward and laid my hand on her arm. It wasn't worth the argument that would ensue. More than anything, I didn't want to put my aunt in the path of Rion's anger. He was hardly reining himself in. I could tell by the taut veins in his forearm and the way his spine was perfectly straight. Occasionally, his index finger would tap against the plush leather.

"Is that what you want, little star?"

I turned toward my uncle and smiled. "I have no doubt I'll be well cared for. Besides, you have Bri to take care of."

My family left an hour later, needing to get Brielle home to rest. They'd been in the waiting room all day. Gods only knew how exhausted they must have felt. But I felt their absence even before they'd left. It loomed overhead like a dark cloud, especially knowing I'd be left alone with Rion.

Would he scold me? Berate me? Tell me I was foolish again? Thoughts swirled around and around, keeping me awake far longer than I should have been. He hadn't spoken since he told my aunt I'd be going home with him, and I didn't know what to say to break the bitter silence, so instead I closed my eyes and fell into a restless sleep.

The next morning, the doctor examined the lingering bruises. "Near perfect!" he remarked. "Have this prescription filled and take them as needed for pain." He handed Rion a small slip of paper with my medication, using what was left of my time here to kiss my husband's ass instead of talking to his actual patient. "Please don't hesitate to call with any questions or concerns."

"Assholes," I murmured under my breath, pushing from the bed.

Rion gave him a tight nod before reaching for a bag underneath his chair I hadn't noticed until now. He set it at the foot of my hospital bed. "I brought you a change of clothes."

I was still clad in my hospital gown and didn't know where the clothes I'd worn during the attack had gone. Opening the leather duffel, I pulled out a pair of soft black leggings, an oversized cashmere sweater, panties, and house slippers.

"Thank you," I whispered, rising and moving to the bathroom to change. It felt fantastic to be in fresh clothes. I brought the sweater to my nostrils and inhaled deeply, lavishing in the clean lavender scent of the detergent. When I was done, Rion pushed off the wall and grabbed my hand before tugging me out the door.

His grip was tight as he intertwined our fingers. I wanted to pull away, but hesitated as we rounded the corner. Just outside the front doors, journalists stared through the glass. When we came into view, we were met with flashing cameras and shouting press. Rion opened an umbrella and pulled me closer. This time, I let him shield me, clinging to his shirt, which still smelled faintly of his cologne.

A black town car slid into the parking area, and security swarmed the area, pushing people back so we could pass. They shouted questions at us like I hadn't just been in a traumatic accident. I don't know why I was surprised; this was their job. It didn't mean I had to like it, though.

But one question I heard above the rest captured my attention.

"Calia! What do you have to say about the recent rumors about Rion's infidelity? Is there trouble in paradise so soon?"

I felt his muscles tense and knew he'd heard it too. Neither of us stopped until we made it to the car. I slid in first, buckling in before Rion followed. Hendrix was up front, giving me a slight nod in the mirror as he pulled away and began driving toward D'Arcy Manor.

There was so much I wanted to ask, but I wasn't sure I was ready for the answers. I knew Rion was no saint. After all, it'd been his idea to see people on the side if we kept it quiet and I heard the female voice on the phone earlier. Most women in Kallistos would sell their souls for a night with him, but he didn't strike me as the type to take a stranger to bed. No, I was willing to bet he picked his partners carefully. It wouldn't surprise me if he had background checks run on someone before agreeing to spend the night with them.

Just the notion of Rion with other women made me sick. Every night I thought about how he'd kissed me in the hall while I pushed my hand between my thighs. The way he gripped my body as if it was the only thing he needed in the world, his tongue tangling with mine, the way he'd ravished my neck. It all sent me over the edge each time. They were wicked, sinful thoughts, but they played repeatedly in my mind.

Neither of us spoke on the way home, but the tension was thick. The space between us was a chasm. I'm sure this was the last place he wanted to be. I wasn't a fool, as he'd claimed. The anger in his body was evident as he vibrated from restraint.

You probably interrupted one hell of a night for him, and she was calling to check on him.

The manor came into view, and he threw open the door before we'd stopped, thundering through the entryway and out of sight. I stared at where he'd just been, resisting the urge to curl in on myself and cry.

I'd save that for when I got to my bedroom.

To his credit, Hendrix helped me out of the car and escorted me up the stairs. He insisted it was no trouble, saying he didn't want me to carry my bags given everything that had happened. His eyes widened as I threw my arms around him in a tight hug. He hesitated only a moment before returning the gesture.

"Thank you," I whispered.

"For what, my dear?"

I fought against the torrent of tears threatening to spill over. "For always being kind, even when you don't know me."

He pulled back and wiped my cheek with his thumb. "It doesn't take time to know someone. You can see everything you need to know when you look into their eyes."

"And what do you see in mine?" I was terrified of his answer.

Hendrix smiled. "Hope, my dear. I see hope."

seventeen

I rested my head on the small pillow attached to my bathtub, enjoying the feel of the silky water along my skin. When I'd gotten back, I'd immediately filled it to the brim with hot water and eucalyptus oil. The minty scent always relaxed me.

Rion hadn't come by to check on me, nor had Jasper. I'd wondered what had happened after I was torn away from him. Did he stay behind to ensure Brielle was safe, or had someone gotten to him at the same time they'd grabbed me? I wanted answers, but there was a possibility I'd never get them.

The bruises on my body were nearly faded, except for a large one stretching down my side to my thigh. I examined the spot on my palm where Jasper had drunk from. As the doctor had said, two crescent markings were permanently etched into my skin. They were jagged and messy, but the dark silver scars would be recognizable.

I hadn't expected it to be so painful. It'd burned and ached from the moment his teeth had sunk into me. Before marrying Rion, I'd done my research on vampyre bites. It was common for married couples to mark each other with their bites. Each one was different somehow, showing the world they were spoken for. The bites themselves weren't supposed to hurt. In fact, many couples took pleasure in the act. Sometimes it was initiated during sex.

It made sense, given the effects Rion's tongue had on my skin at our wedding ceremony. Even if it hadn't been a true bite, the small pulls I'd felt had been euphoric.

Before our wedding, I'd wondered if we would mark one another. Once I'd spoken to him, however, I'd realized that would never happen. He wouldn't want that on his skin, not when he planned to secretly live his life as a bachelor.

Yet, when he'd found out Jasper's mark wouldn't fade from my skin, he'd seemed angry. Was it because Jasper had tasted me first—some primal need to conquer and own my body, even though he wanted nothing to do with me?

The door to my bathroom swung open, and I looked up into storm cloud eyes. "Get out!" I shrieked, sinking lower into the water to hide my body.

He froze with his hand on the doorknob, lips parted in shock. Without saying a word, he turned and shut the door. "What the fuck?" I muttered, stepping out of the water and drying myself quickly.

My clothes were in the other room, but a long, viridian robe hung next to the door. I grabbed it, wrapping my body in the soft fabric before stepping next door. Rion sat perched on my bed, his arms crossed. He still wore the same tight expression as earlier, and I wondered if he always had that look on his face.

I leaned against the dresser, exhaustion weighing me down. "If you've come to fight, Rion, I don't have the energy. Can we do this tomorrow?"

Suddenly, he was on his feet. He stormed toward me, placing his arms on either side of my body so I was trapped. I fought to control my breathing as his burning stare bore into me. Every alarm bell went off in my head, warning me that this man was dangerous. But I couldn't bring myself to push him away.

"Why do you think I do not care?" he asked harshly, inhaling the eucalyptus scent clinging to my skin.

"W-What?"

"You heard me, love. Why do you think I do not care?" Each word was heavily emphasized, dragging them out to prove his point.

"Because you don't." I looked away, unable to bear the heavy weight of his scrutinizing gaze.

His hand shot out and gripped my chin, pulling me back toward him. We were inches apart, our breaths mingling in a way that made me dizzy. Because everything about this man was intoxicating, and I wanted to drown in him.

"Do not presume to know my thoughts."

I tore myself from his hold and pushed him away. "I don't need to presume anything, *husband*. Your actions are what prove your thoughts. You took a fucking phone call from another woman while you were having a conversation with me."

He dared to laugh, causing my temper to flare. I pointed at the door, trying to smother the rage clawing to get out. "Get out, Rion."

He stepped closer, his face darkening. "No."

I stormed forward and pushed again, but he didn't budge. He was unmovable, a statue of perfection whose purpose was to show me everything I could never have. "*Get Out.*"

Rion leaned forward, brushing my nose with his own. "Do I make you angry, *wife*?"

Again, I pushed at his chest. "You infuriate me, *husband*."

"Good. Then you know but a fraction of what you do to me."

And then he kissed me. *Hard.*

It was bruising and passionate and burning—all the things our first kiss had been, only intensified by both our tempers. We tangled for dominance. My hands weaved through his hair as his traveled low to grip my ass. He groaned against my lips as I tightened my hold, picking me up and setting me on the sturdy dresser behind me.

He ground his erection against the apex of my things. I cried out, remembering the only thing separating our bodies were his clothes and my robe. I hadn't put on panties. Oh gods, he could slip in if he wanted to. It'd be so easy.

As if Rion could read my mind, he slid a hand between us, quickly finding how much my body wanted him. "Your anger is doing wicked things to this sweet pussy, Calia. You cannot deny it, can you?"

His mouth slid down my neck, biting and sucking as my groan of frustration turned to one of passion. Everything he did, everywhere he touched, set my skin aflame. I needed him, even though I'd regret it once we were done.

Rion pulled back and gripped my throat with his hand, squeezing. "Answer me."

"Yes."

Dark eyes turned to molten silver as he lunged forward, capturing my mouth again. I fumbled with the buttons on his shirt, ripping them apart when they refused to cooperate. As my hands touched his skin, he let out a sharp inhale. I'd landed on his scar. The raised lines were soft compared to the rest of his hard body, allowing me to feel its expanse.

"How did it happen?" I whispered, tracing the mark.

"I don't want to talk about it, love. In fact, I don't want to talk at all. I only want to hear the little sounds you make when you come." Suddenly, he dropped to his knees before me, gripping my thighs tightly as he pulled them apart. Embarrassment pushed through the lust, and I fought against his hold. His silver gaze met mine. "Why are you trying to hide from me?"

He sat back on his heels, raising his eyebrow when an answer didn't come. If I was honest, there were many reasons for my hiding. Stretch marks and cellulite marred my skin, something I'd fought against since childhood. My hips were wide and my thighs constantly rubbed together when I walked. There was no makeup on my face, highlighting the red tone it always pulled without concealer. I braced myself for the rejection that would surely come once he saw what I did every time I looked in the mirror—how the mile long list of imperfections would void any value I could offer a lover.

The women he'd been with were beautiful—*perfect* —while the list of my flaws would run a mile long.

Realization flashed in his eyes before he gripped me tighter and yanked my legs back open. "I should kill every person who made you feel as if you were not enough."

Before I could respond, his tongue lapped at my slick entrance. I gripped his hair tightly in my fists as he pulled me closer to him, burying his face between my thighs. Every move he made felt reverent, his fingers wrapped around me tight as though I was the only thing holding him down.

My head fell back, and I moaned, moving my hips in encouragement. Each horrible thought fell away from my mind, leaving me grounded in this moment with him as one of his hands came around and played with my clit.

I looked down my body, met with his striking eyes as he watched my pleasure peak into an earth-shattering orgasm. He was frozen, as though he didn't want to miss a single moment of the way he wrecked me.

Rion sat up and captured my mouth in a searing kiss. I tasted myself on his tongue, surprised at how it only made me crave him more. My fingers flew to his pants, tearing at the zipper where his cock was hard and waiting.

"Fuck, Calia," he hissed as I gripped him in my hand. For just a moment, I felt powerful. It was stupid; I'd been with lovers in the past, but never one like Rion. There was something euphoric about bringing such a powerful man to his knees for my pleasure and the sounds he made at my touch.

At that moment, Rion had given me the greatest gift, and I hated how it made me feel. It gave me a taste of something I didn't know if I would ever have again.

"Do you want me?" I asked him, tugging roughly at his cock. His deep growl sent tendrils of pleasure rolling through me, but I didn't relent. "Answer me, Rion. Do. You. Want. Me?" I used his words against him, reveling in how his eyes flashed.

"Yes," he said through gritted teeth.

"Yes, what?"

"Yes, I fucking want you." Without warning, he picked me up, carrying me to my bed. I let out a small gasp as I fell, landing amidst the plush bedding. He stood over me, chest bare and pants unzipped. Somehow, he looked even more enticing than before because I knew *I* had been the one to dismantle his perfect appearance.

Rion began to crawl onto the bed, and I shuddered at the desire in his gaze. The full force of it weighed on me, making me yearn for his touch. He tugged himself free and positioned the head of his cock at my entrance while I lay open for him, waiting for my ruination.

But the moment was fleeting as a knock sounded on my door—a soft feminine voice following quickly. "Rion?" We both froze. "Are you in there?"

eighteen

I pushed at Rion's chest, scrambling away as fast as possible to escape him while he sat back on his knees. His gaze was fixed on the spot I had occupied—the dip my body had left behind in the bedding.

I clutched at my robe, covering myself. "*Who is that?*" I hissed, pointing at the door. He didn't look at me, nor did he need to.

His silence told me everything I needed to know.

As another knock sounded, Rion pushed off the bed and grabbed his shirt from near the dresser. I could still feel the hard planes of his chest, the rigidness of his cock, and the desperation of his lips as I watched him leave. But where those had given small surges of pleasure before, they now settled at the bottom of my stomach to remain an agonizing reminder of what could have been.

"Ri—" the voice called, but was interrupted as Rion

ripped open the door and grasped her upper arm. She looked past him, eyes flashing with something I couldn't quite place as I still held my robe shut.

He said nothing as he left, leaving me in silence. I ran to the door, unable to stop myself from pressing an ear to the wood to listen to their departure.

"What are you doing here?" he snapped.

"I have been waiting in your room for over an hour. It is not like you to be late—"

"So, you thought knocking on my wife's door would be a good idea?" There was something venomous in the way he asked his question.

The woman laughed, sending chills down my spine. "It isn't as though your relationship with her is real."

She yelped, not from pain but surprise. "Allow me to make myself clear. Never go near her room again. Do not look at her. Do not talk to her. Do not breathe the same air as her." After a pause, he continued in a low voice. I almost didn't hear his words. "She is far better than you and I."

THE SUN PEEKED THROUGH THE CURTAINS, CASTING A muted glow across the room. I felt even more exhausted than I had in the hospital. Given that I'd spent most of the night tossing, turning, cursing the gods, and crying, I wasn't entirely surprised.

I'd been at war with my mind since Rion had left.

One moment, I was berating myself for believing he might've wanted me, and the other was spent remembering the awful color of the prison jumpsuits I'd wear if I was found guilty of his murder.

I'd always struggled with my self-worth, but until now, I thought I'd gotten a handle on those disturbing thoughts. I'd watched women tear themselves apart over their insecurities, myself included. Something about Rion's blasé demeanor had me questioning everything. From the moment I saw him, I knew he'd be the one to turn my world upside and shatter the ground beneath my feet.

I didn't want to be a woman drooling over a man who'd never want her, but dammit, his tongue had felt good against my skin. I'd been so angry last night that I hadn't felt the ache he had left behind until now.

I slid a hand underneath my t-shirt, groping my breast roughly to mirror how he'd been with me last night, while the other trailed down my soft tummy to rest between my thighs. I ached for Rion, hating how much he made me want him as I soaked through the fabric of my panties.

Gods, it felt good, but it wasn't enough. Even as I circled my clit, I wanted more. I wanted rough, calloused fingers caressing my skin—for them to part my flesh and dig inside me, forcing me to give up my release. To know that he craved my pleasure as much as I craved experiencing it. And at the peak of it all, he would spear me with his molten gaze, and that would be the last thing I saw as I crested the wave of my orgasm and rode it out.

I ground against my hand shamelessly, working myself into a frenzy until a slight sheen of sweat beaded my brow. I couldn't hold back the small whimpers, letting them fill the room and break the silence.

What would Rion say if he walked in to find me like this? Would he turn his back and leave, or would he stay and finish what he started? Because all of this was his fault. He'd stormed into my room. He'd kissed me. He'd left me wanton and needy. And now I had to take matters into my own hands, chasing a euphoria I knew would feel nothing like having him hard and pulsing inside me.

With a final cry, I lost myself. My back arched off the bed, legs trapping my hand between my thighs as I rode out the last wave. I was panting, unsure if I'd done the right thing, but knowing I wouldn't have made a different choice if I was given the option.

No, I wanted that pleasure, even if it came with pain.

My phone pinged, and I reached to pick it up to find Bri's shining face. She'd sent me a selfie holding two cups and a bag of pastries from our favorite coffee shop, telling me she was on her way. I threw on a pair of leggings and a sweater before ambling downstairs.

I bypassed the kitchen, heading straight to the atrium on the outskirts of the massive lawn. The entire building was encased in enchanted glass that allowed the vampyres of the household to see the sun. I would sometimes sit there in the afternoons, drinking tea and watching the dogs run free as they were now.

Five massive black beasts bounded toward me, nearly knocking me to the ground as they pawed for my attention. "Sit. Sit!" I chided half-hearted, laughing as I pushed them away. "Have you missed me, babies?"

They followed obediently as I took a seat next to Anya. Each one waited patiently for me to greet them. "Nyx. Aurelia. Enyo. Poppy. Dex. Has Anya been spoiling you?"

I looked pointedly at the older woman, who held up her hands and smiled before pushing a plate of cookies my way. "They'll never tell," she said, giving me a quick once over. "How are you feeling?"

"Fine," I lied. "Still sore, but I'm thankful for the fresh air."

She scrunched her nose. "Let's say I believe that bullshit you're spouting; the way the master of the house has been stomping around all morning tells me something different."

I picked up a chocolate chip cookie and nibbled mindlessly instead of answering her question. Rion's issues had nothing to do with me. I'm sure he was upset at losing the moral high ground, given his mistress came calling while he was seconds away from ruining my body completely.

"I don't know why his panties are in a twist, if that's what you're asking."

Anya rolled her eyes. "Keep telling yourself that, girl. Maybe one day you'll believe it."

We both jerked our heads at the sound of a high pitch squeal behind us. Brielle ran up to us with her arms stuffed with breakfast snacks and coffee. I stood to help her, but she quickly tossed the food on the table and sank to her knees amongst the dogs, ignoring me altogether.

"OH. MY. GODS. THESE ARE THE CUTEST PUPPIES EVER!" she exclaimed as each dog clamored over the other to seek her attention. Soon, Brielle was completely submerged underneath them, only an occasional glimpse of her hand to be seen.

"You two are going to ruin them forever!" Anya chided, sifting through the bag for a lemon square.

I pointed at Anya. "Don't pretend it's our fault. You're just as guilty."

"I don't know what you're talking about."

"Do too."

"Oh, just like you don't know what your husband is pissed off about?" She snapped her fingers, and the dogs backed away from Brielle, tails wagging and tongues lolling.

Brielle pouted. "Why'd you do that? Death by puppy cuddles is at the top of my list of ways to die."

Anya shook her head. "You are both strange girls."

I bumped her shoulder. "And here you are, hanging out with us."

"Technically, I was here before either of you showed up. So much for enjoying the peace and quiet."

Brielle pushed off the ground, taking a seat across from us. We quickly laid out the spread of food she'd brought, eating with our mouths full and laughing to our heart's content. After an hour, one of the dogs lifted its head and stared toward the main house. It wasn't long until each dog sat at attention, their hackles raised.

My stomach dropped as the woman from last night walked out of the back door and began her trek through the hall toward us. Her black hair was cropped into a short bob that barely brushed the tops of her shoulders. It swung with each step she took, yet not a hair was out of place. She looked like the type of woman I could picture Rion with—beautiful, statuesque, and perfect in every way.

"*Shit*," Anya muttered.

Brielle sat up straighter, pushing her hair over her shoulder. "Please tell me that's not—"

"It is," I said, forcing feelings of inadequacy into a tiny box inside my mind. Even the dogs sensed my irritation, their ears flattening back before emitting a low growl.

The woman stopped short, looking down at the dogs with disdain before forcing a smile and continuing toward us. She wobbled slightly, the heels of her shoes sinking into the fake grass. "Good morning. I was wondering if I could speak with Calia."

Anya and Brielle looked at me, unsure if they should intervene or let it play out. Still, their eyes widened as I nodded and stood from the table. "Okay." I followed her to a small grove of trees, obscuring us from the sun. Her sharp, blue eyes bore into me, scanning me for weakness. I wasn't short, but she was at least four inches taller than I was in her shoes. "How can I help you?"

Her gaze dipped down my body, but I stood up a little straighter instead of shrinking in on myself as I wanted to. "I wanted to introduce myself, seeing as we will likely become... *acquainted* while you are here. My name is Senna." She held out her hand, but I didn't take it. Instead, I stared down at it and back up to her face. Her smile faltered, but she quickly covered it up with a chuckle. "I knew I would like you."

"What did you want with my husband last night?"

She waved her hand. "We had some unfinished business to take care of. Nothing to worry yourself about."

"Seeing as you pulled him from my bed, I'd consider it my issue."

Senna leaned in, her lips twisted in a knowing smirk. "If he could be pulled so easily from your bed, perhaps that is your bigger issue." Her words hurt, hitting their intended target as she'd hoped, yet she didn't stop. "He is not easily satisfied. I have known him for a very, *very* long time. I know what he likes, what he craves, what he needs." She clicked her tongue. "You do not."

"You know all of these things, and yet it isn't you who wears his ring."

She narrowed her eyes. For the first time since we began talking, I felt a twinge of fear as she lifted her lip in a snarl and displayed the sharp fangs hiding underneath. "You will not last. You are fleeting, and there will come a day where I will be by his side."

"Senna!"

We turned toward the house to see Rion pushing open the large glass door and striding out. A button-down white shirt fit his figure snugly, tucked into a pair of black slacks. His sleeves were rolled up, showing off his impressive muscles. I could still feel the pressure of his body against my own, seeking out my pleasure as if he, and he alone, could draw it from me. But it was the severe expression he wore on his face that made that salacious flashback come to a glaring halt.

Rion stopped next to me, placing his hand on my lower back. The simple touch set me on fire, and we weren't even connecting skin-to-skin. "Rion, what a surprise!" Senna said, chuckling nervously. "I thought you had business in the city?"

"I canceled my meetings."

Her brows furrowed. "But they were important."

"Not as important as ensuring my wife is well-rested and cared for." His hand slid around my waist, and he gently pulled me to him before kissing my temple. "After all, she was just attacked and nearly killed."

What the fuck was happening? Did he just... kiss me?

Senna tracked the gesture, her lips thinning as she watched us. "Right. Of course. Well, I suppose I should be getting back to my job now—*especially since I have meetings to reschedule.*" She dipped her head before hastily retreating toward the house.

Neither of us moved until she was gone. Not that I could've even if I wanted to. His hold was absolute, crushing my body to his own until I cleared my throat.

He stepped away, pushing his hands into the pocket of his slacks.

My confusion bled into annoyance as he stared at me expectantly. "What do you want?" I snapped, pushing past him toward my friends.

He followed, but was soon stopped by the five giant dogs who stood in a protective stance before us. Anya hid her chuckle behind a cough as Rion blinked down at his beasts. "What have you done to my animals?"

I leaned forward, giving Poppy a scratch behind her ears. Seeing Rion after what happened last night soured my mood. Darkness crept into my mind, winding around my thoughts like thorn-covered vines. He'd embarrassed me, made me feel vulnerable and stupid in a moment of weakness. I don't know why I thought he would want me when the alternative outmatched me in every way.

And why had he put on a show in front of Senna, as though he didn't leave my room last night to fuck her? Though she hadn't said the words, her insinuation was clear.

"Perhaps they like me better than you."

"Nonsense. They are highly trained animals, and you've turned them into—" he gestured around him "—lap dogs."

Poppy let out a low growl. "Looks like they offer their protection to those of us who are worthy," I said with a chuckle.

"*Damn...*" Brielle whispered, causing Anya to slap

the back of her head. "Oh, right! We'll, uh, leave you guys."

They scurried off toward Anya's cottage, disappearing through the thicket of trees outside the atrium. Meanwhile, Rion and I stared at one another. I didn't know what to say or how to start a conversation with him. Not after what happened. What was I supposed to ask? If he'd enjoyed his evening with his mistress?

No thanks.

"Are you not going to speak to me?" he asked after a long beat of silence.

I turned toward him, crossing my arms. Now was as good of a time as any other. And I'd read too many romance books to know that not communicating wouldn't end well. "What would you like to speak about, dear husband? Should we talk about the apparent rumors of you having a mistress that were shouted at us while we left the hospital? Or what about the fact that you made me come on your face and were mere moments away from fucking me when a woman pulled you from my bed?"

"None of them are true."

"Don't lie to me. I'm not oblivious, Rion. I saw the way she looked at you. The two of you have fucked—many times before if her words are anything to go by." I didn't give him a chance to respond, already feeling my cheeks flush with embarrassment. I stood and tried to pass him, but he grasped my wrist and pulled me back. "Let me go, Rion."

He paused, nostrils flaring as he looked at my hand.

Then, a wicked smile spread on his lips. "It seems as though I am not needed to make you come. You are more than capable of doing that on your own."

It only took a second to realize what he was talking about. I ripped my wrist away from him, clasping my hands behind my back. "You flatter yourself by assuming it was you on my mind, husband."

His eyes darkened, a muscle feathering in his jaw. "Who, pray tell, were you imagining, wife? Give me their name."

"Why?"

He leaned in closer. "So I can kill them."

Oh, gods. It shouldn't have been sexy. His words should have scared me because I knew he wasn't joking. But against my better judgment, I loved this possessive side of him. And that made me want to provoke him further. "I thought we could see other people. Weren't those your words?"

Rion tilted his head. "And what if I want to renegotiate the terms of our relationship?"

I huffed. "I'm pretty sure we have to have a relationship first for terms to renegotiate..."

"We have a relationship."

"No, we don't," I said, laughing. "And why would I want one with you when, quite frankly, you've been a dick from the moment I met you? We have nothing in common. We have no similar desires—"

"If we are talking about the desires that had you plunging your hand between those pretty thighs, I can confirm they are the same."

I blushed, scowling up at him. "Stop it. Don't say things like that."

He frowned. "And why not?"

There was one thing I could do to shut him down. If we continued this conversation, he could sweet-talk me into anything he wanted. That was the last thing I needed, even if I knew it would be worth the frustration.

"Where's Jasper?"

Rion's eyes narrowed into slits, his body going rigid. "Why?" he asked coldly.

"Because I haven't seen him since the attack. Consider me curious." Absentmindedly, my finger traced the raised lines of my new scar. It'd been the wrong thing to do—Rion's line of sight zeroed in on the slight movement.

He stepped closer, backing me into a tree. "Was it him?"

I couldn't think with him this close. The faint hint of whiskey on his breath had me leaning in without a second thought. I wanted him to kiss me, get me drunk from his lips and tongue. "What?" I breathed. I couldn't remember his question.

"Was. It. Him?"

I blinked, looking up at him through my lashes. "And what if it was?"

"If it was, then I am delighted to know he is being disciplined for not protecting you."

"What do you mean?" I asked, apprehension making my skin crawl.

Rion placed his finger under my chin and tilted my

head up. "Did you truly think there would be no punishment for his actions? He did not keep you safe. He bit you. You were kidnapped and then nearly died. I should have killed him. I have killed others for less." He looked away, lips pursed and angry.

"Why do you care what happens to me?" I whispered, feeling foolish for the way my stupid heart fluttered at his words.

He was silent for a long time, locking us in a moment we didn't know how to break. I wasn't sure why I couldn't get my question out. Initially, he'd acted cold and indifferent, wanting nothing to do with me. Now, he was ready to redefine our relationship and kill his best friend. "I wish I knew," he said softly, meeting my gaze.

I nodded my head. It wasn't much, but maybe it was enough to try and bridge the gap between us. "Alright. We'll start there. But I have questions, and I need answers."

nineteen

"Uh, where are we going?" I asked, gripping the railing tightly as I followed Rion down a small stone staircase beneath the mansion. When I'd told him I wanted answers, he asked me to follow him. I did so without question. I assumed he wouldn't lure me into a cellar to kill me.

Now, I was having second thoughts.

"I am not going to kill you, Calia. You are more valuable to me alive than dead," he said with a dark chuckle.

"Is that supposed to be reassuring?" If anything, it was creepy—the way he nearly read my mind. Gods. It would be mortifying to find out he'd been able to do that this entire time. But Rion didn't answer and just continued his slow descent. "And have you ever thought of installing better lights? Because this isn't—"

I stumbled over my own feet, losing my balance and plunging forward. I held my breath, waiting for impact, but it never came. Instead of hitting the floor, I was enveloped by strong arms, tugging me closer to him. "You are rather clumsy."

"Well, if you had better lighting down here, it wouldn't be a problem," I snapped, pushing back and standing straight. The dim sconces on the wall cast a gloomy shadow over half of his face, highlighting the thickening stubble along his chin. I'd never been a fan of facial hair on men before, but something about how it looked on him made him seem distinguished. And the way it felt as it scraped the inside of my thighs was sinful...

His hold temporarily tightened before he cleared his throat and stepped back, offering me his elbow. I stared at it for only a second before grabbing ahold of it. It was stupid. Every time I touched him, it sent a thrill through my body. Which was counterproductive when I was trying so hard to stay away from him.

The deeper we went, the more pungent the stench of mildew became, overpowering the sweetness of Rion's body. Water droplets fell from the walls and ceiling, creating puddles on the ground below.

The stairs finally gave way to a narrow space—open, save for a cylindrical object standing tall in the middle of the room. It reminded me of a coffin wrapped in chains. There was a small, covered window at eye level, but it appeared welded shut. Rion observed me as I stepped into the room. I had a sick feeling I knew what this place was, a not-so-distant memory becoming clear in my mind.

He took a few steps in front of where I stood. I didn't know if I wanted to hear what he had to say, but curiosity won out, and I stayed silent. "Our home has gone through countless renovations over the years, modernizing as the times changed, but this," he paused, peering at the iron structure, "has never changed. The room was used for many things—a prison, a slaughter-house, an asylum. As our numbers grew, my ancestor Arowan built this to punish his children when their cravings became too insatiable. It completely removes you from your senses, depriving you of everything but oxygen. He would not give Calix yet another reason to label us as monsters. "

He began circling me slowly, akin to a predator stalking its prey. The muted lights above cast a subtle glow onto his skin, making him appear even more menacing than he was. But despite the darkness, his eyes still sparkled.

"The first week is the worst. Everything is height-ened—your emotions, your desires, your urges. The body craves the necessities it is being deprived of." He stopped before me, his breath skating along the back of my neck and sending shivers down my spine. "Can you imagine what that could drive someone to do, love?"

The sound of fists beating against iron broke through the spell Rion held me in. I jumped back, slam-ming into his hard chest. His arms looped around my waist, holding me close.

"Calia?" Jasper called. His voice was scratchy and hoarse, barely audible through the barrier. "Calia, are you there?" I couldn't speak, couldn't think. Just hearing the pitiful sounds he was making had nausea turning in the pit of my stomach. "Please forgive me. Please help me."

Rion moved toward a small panel I hadn't noticed before. He pressed a button, and the window slot opened. It was silent. "Come closer."

At Rion's command, I stepped closer, even though I didn't want to. I shook my head furiously. "No, stop." But he didn't. He watched as I fought against whatever magic worked held me in its grasp.

When I was no more than two steps away, Jasper's face appeared through the small window. He was beaten and bruised. A large gash marred his cheek, the wound dirty and scabbed over. The blood vessels in one of his eyes had burst, surrounding his pupil with crimson. His lips were crusted from dehydration.

I spun and looked at Rion, whose gaze had darkened. "This is cruel."

"No," he said in a low tone. "This is retribution. He did not protect you as he was sworn to do." My husband stepped forward. "He *marked* you."

"I did not mean to," Jasper cried. "I did not even want to drink from her. Tell him!"

Before I could try, Rion bared his teeth and growled, causing Jaspers to shrink back in the confined space. "Watch your mouth, friend. You do not command her."

Suddenly, Rion's rage made sense. *That's* why he cared. It had nothing to do with me but rather what the symbolism behind Jasper's bite would mean to others.

His wife was marked by another man. No matter the circumstances, that's all anyone would see.

Jasper's mewls became louder, filling the room until I could no longer comprehend the thoughts racing through my mind. He clawed at the container until the smell of copper filled the room. He sucked at the tips of his fingers, a man crazed for nourishment in any form.

I stepped back, clutching my stomach. "I don't want to see anymore." Rion pressed the button, closing the window and muffling Jasper's cries. I met his star-flecked gaze, unsure of the hunger I saw in it. "Why did you show this to me?"

"So that perhaps you can understand the depth of my confusion regarding you. I have lived over 200 years, love. Nothing, not even my desire for blood, has driven me mad as you do. It is infuriating and senseless." His hands curled into tight fists at his side as if he was stopping himself from reaching out and touching me.

Did I want that after what I just saw? Would I welcome the feel of him on my skin? There was only one way to find out, and I had to find the strength to allow that kind of vulnerability with this man.

"Were you angry about the mark because of what others may think? Or is it because he's tasted me, and you haven't?" My question was bold, but I needed to know if this was a superficial attraction or if true feelings lurked underneath all the bullshit.

He lurched forward, wrapping his hand around my throat and pulling me toward him. His touch was rough, but he kept his grip loose so I could breathe. "Do not remind me of that." Rion's lips were close to my own. "For it makes me want to drag him out and kill him with my bare hands."

"Now you know how I felt."

He tilted his head, studying me. "What?"

I leaned forward. "Did you fuck Senna last night after you left my room?"

"No," he said without hesitation. "She and I—we have a complicated past. One I hope to share with you one day, but for now, you must know that I have not taken or touched another woman since the day we wed."

"What about all the nights you spent out of the house?"

His forehead touched my own. "It was so I would not crawl into your bed as you have crawled under my skin."

I closed my eyes against the swarm of butterflies taking flight in my stomach. I'd wanted a chance to grow and explore these confusing emotions plaguing me, and here he was, offering the opportunity to me on a silver platter.

But these were just words, and I couldn't trust him unless those words became actions. Everything he'd done or said up until this point worked against him. I didn't want to be one of those women who fell in the villains' arms without question. Because there was no mistaking Rion as a hero. He was brash and often cruel with his words and intentions. I'd heard stories about his ruthlessness and his pursuit of wicked fantasies.

"I don't trust you," I whispered. I hated how the words tasted bitter on my tongue, but it didn't change how I felt. The fact was, I had no reason to put my faith in this man who had been nothing short of a nightmare since I met him. Nor did I even know what I wanted from him.

"Then I try to will change that," he promised. I saw the struggle in his eyes. For someone so used to being in charge, he was waging an internal battle. For what, though, I wasn't sure. "By telling you what we know about the people that attacked you."

twenty

Rion led me from the underground chamber to his office, taking care to navigate me through the darkness so there were no more accidents. The space was just as I'd imagined, with walls of deepest blue and dark hardwood floors. Two large windows comprised most of the back wall, offering a view of the Odesza below. They framed his desk and bathed the room in natural lighting, which was quickly dimming with the setting sun.

"The view is beautiful," I said in awe, momentarily distracted from the confusing feelings churning around in my head.

"Yes. It is."

The door clicked behind me, and I turned to find Rion leaning against the wall. His gaze roamed over me, darkening with each sweep. There was something about the moment that felt pivotal. Beneath the haze of lust clouding our emotions, there was something *more*, something reckless that could ruin both our lives. There was no explanation, no tangible evidence. Instead, it was something I simply *knew*. The knowledge was in my very being, and nothing could change it.

He pushed off the wall and stalked toward me, clasping my hands between his palms. "I do not have the answer to every question, but I will share with you what I know." I nodded. No matter how much I wanted to demand information, I knew he wouldn't know everything. Such little time had passed since the accident. But what he did know? I craved that almost as much as I craved him.

Rion gestured toward his desk, and I sat in a plush leather chair while he walked around and grabbed a thick folder. He returned and sat next to me before scattering photographs along the wood.

My stomach churned as I saw the horror depicted below. Each photo contained pictures of mutilated bodies, their blood-soaked skin making it hard to see what I was truly looking at. I covered my mouth. "My gods. What is this?"

"This is every single person who was there the day of your attack."

I turned to him. "You did this?"

He lifted his shoulder in casual arrogance. "I had help." I attempted to protest, and he held up his hand. "You did not see your body after the accident, Calia. You were beaten and bruised. So much blood matted your hair to your body... I thought—"

But he didn't need to vocalize what he thought because it was clear. He believed I was dead. But what about his own body and the burns that had marred his skin when I'd woken up? Had those been injuries he'd received from tearing into my attackers?

Swallowing my nausea and confusion toward his care, I turned to stare and the pictures. "What did you find out before you killed them?"

Rion leaned back in his chair. "Very little, unfortunately. They refused to divulge information, regardless of the method of torture. Whoever is behind this has trained them well."

"So, we know nothing?"

"Not quite. While they were silent on who they were, there is something linking them together." I was quiet while Rion sorted through the images until he found what he sought. "At first, we assumed it was an attack orchestrated by a disgruntled rogue. Not everyone was thrilled to see us join. But when this group was brought to us, it was comprised of an array of beings—vampyres, fae, witches, and even a few mortals. Which means this is something we haven't seen before."

"How do we find what we do not know?"

Rion tapped a spot on one of the pictures. "Each body was marked by this symbol. Some were tattooed on, while others were burned or carved. Do you recognize it?" I shook my head, unable to speak. It looked like the blade of a sword, except where a pommel would be, there was a slender diamond. "Even I did not know. Anya's father, however, was a noted historian. She still has many of his old books and searched them for answers."

"And did she find them?" I asked, nervously playing with the sleeve of my sweater.

"Yes and no. She could not procure a name. Still, she did find references to this symbol being etched into the walls of the old fae palace before it was destroyed. According to her father's notes, it is believed to symbolize protection. From what, we do not know."

I thrummed my fingers along my thigh, hoping to expel the nervous energy coursing through my body. "What happens now? Is this where you vow to protect me?" I joked, but it fell flat. We both knew there was a glimmer of a confession behind my words.

Rion grasped my hand, intertwining my fingers with his to stop the fidgeting. "This is where I teach you to protect yourself. Your uncle instilled the basics of combat with you, yes?" I nodded. "Good. I would like you to have him train you further, at least once a week."

"And what will you do?"

He leaned in slowly, grazing my thigh with the tips of his fingers as he dragged our hands along my skin. His gaze dropped to my lips, which parted for him quickly. "I will teach you how to read people and stop them from reading you."

"Am I that obvious?"

He smirked, sending shivers down my spine as he stroked a fingertip along my skin. "I know you have wanted to fuck me since you laid eyes on me." I let out a breath I'd been holding, knowing deep down it was true.

Denying it would have been useless. "And despite how much you are trying to hate me, you do not." His other arm rested on the back of the chair behind me. All I could focus on was the small circles he made with his thumb on my hand. "Would you have let me pull that pretty dress up around your hips, love? Would you have let me feast upon your flesh in that wedding chapel, knowing you were only moments away from being mine?"

I whimpered at his words, clasping my thighs together as if it could stop the ache Rion had caused. "Yes," I whispered, leaning in. I loathed the admission, but it didn't change the truth. "I would have." The leather seat back groaned under his grip as he tightened his hold. It thrilled me, knowing he was just as affected as I was. The silver in his eyes became more prominent, spreading through his irises like a branching sea of stars. "Tell me more."

"What if I showed you instead?" Before I could answer, he moved and gripped my thighs. He placed me atop his desk, the outline of his erection pressed against my aching center. His mouth descended on mine in unleashed carnal need. His hands sought purchase along my ass, pulling me closer until there was no space between us.

Sex and lust were things I could rationalize in my mind. They were my body's reaction to what he was doing. I wanted him and he wanted me. It didn't have to come with greater meanings, even if I knew it would— but I shut that portion of my mind off for now.

I clawed at his shirt, popping the buttons carelessly. Again, I was met with the savage scar across his pectoral. "Will you tell me who hurt you?"

And just like the last time, he answered, "Later."

Needy lips moved to my neck as I fumbled with his belt, struggling to unlatch it. Suddenly, his phone rang. Rion continued his assault while I paused. "Do you need to get that?"

"No."

The ringing stopped, only to start up again.

"I really think you should—"

"*No.*"

On the third time, I reached over and picked up the phone. The name Rowena flashed on the screen. As soon as he saw it, he plucked it from my fingers and answered. "What?" he snapped.

I couldn't make out the words from the other end, but Rion pinched the bridge of his nose before brusquely hanging up and tossing it back on the desk. He sat in the chair I'd been in earlier, running his hands through his hair.

"What is it?"

He sighed. "My sister, who also called me while you were at the hospital, is coming to the city earlier than expected for the blood moon celebration. I was hoping to have you all to myself a while longer."

I blinked. "It was... your sister on the phone that day?"

"It was," he said, not even trying to hide his smirk.

I didn't fight my smile, sliding down and straddling

his lap. Torturing him would be my new favorite pastime. His hands ran up my back, pulling me closer, snarling as I deliberately applied pressure to his aching hardness. "What a shame you didn't take advantage of your good fortune earlier. Think of all the surfaces we could have christened."

I pecked his cheek and stood up, straightening my clothes. His eyes widened. "What are you doing? We are not finished here," he said.

"Unfortunately for you, we are. I need to call my uncle and arrange these training dates, and you need to make me dinner."

"Is that so?" he replied, lips kicking up in a smirk I wanted both to kiss and slap.

I nodded. "Indeed it is. Consider it a part of your husbandly duties. You have much to make up for."

Rion swatted my ass as he stood, herding me to the door. As much as I wanted to stay in this moment with him, I couldn't stop thinking about that symbol and the fact I'd seen it before.

Among my uncle's tattoos.

twenty-one

I returned to my room before dinner, telling Rion I wanted to change clothes and call my uncle. One was the truth, and the other a lie, but what was I supposed to say? "I think my uncle may be a part of a secret society trying to kidnap me?"

No, thank you.

It was just a coincidence, wasn't it? I'm sure the symbol had a multitude of meanings. Just because it belonged to a group didn't mean that was the entire reason for its creation, right? I'd seen it before while learning about the symbolism of the wooden stake. Though mortals thought it to be the one thing that would keep them safe from vampyres, it did nothing but incapacitate them for a few minutes. Still, before it became associated with destruction, it belonged to the builders and harvesters as a pivotal tool in their daily arsenal.

Either way, I wouldn't know until I learned more about the symbol and what it meant. My uncle was not from Kallistos. Perhaps it held a different meaning to his people, but I wouldn't know unless I asked.

Not that I could come right out with the question. Castor was far more cunning than most people I knew and would see my question for what it was.

Fear.

It didn't matter because this was all hypothetical. Even though my uncle bore the mark, I knew he wouldn't harm me. In fact, he'd taught me to protect myself from an early age. Why would he do so if he planned to kidnap me?

I stared down at the phone in my hand, fighting the bile rising in my throat at the thought of his betrayal. I'd lost many people, but my aunt and uncle were my constant. They were there for me through thick and thin, better or worse, victory or destruction. If they'd only been raising me for slaughter, I'd welcome death. I wouldn't want to live in a world so cruel.

I pressed his name, bringing the phone to my ear. It rang for so long that I assumed he wouldn't pick up, but his cheery voice came through the line at the last minute. "Little star," he greeted. "This is a surprise. Are you well?"

"I'm feeling much better than I should be, given my injuries."

"And are you being properly cared for? Just say the word, and I will bring you home."

Do you mean kidnap me? I couldn't help the thought. "No, I'm fine. I promise. But I did have a favor to ask."

"What is it?"

I paced in front of my bed, fidgeting with the hem of my shirt. "Uncle, I want to be prepared for the next attack, and you're the best warrior I know."

He was silent on the other line for a beat before answering. "What makes you think there will be another attack, little star?"

"I don't know. It's just a feeling I have. They've already tried twice. What's to stop them from trying again?

Once more, that silence stretched before I heard a heavy sigh from the other line. "Of course, little star. We can resume your training if it makes you feel safer. When would you like to begin?" We quickly made plans to begin over the weekend. Before hanging up, my uncle added, "I will see you at the mayor's party tomorrow evening."

I groaned. I'd hoped the stupid thing would've been canceled. "That's still happening?"

My uncle chuckled. "Yes. They postponed it a few days given your *accident*, but now that you are well, it's in full swing again."

We chatted more before finally saying our goodbyes. I still couldn't believe he could have anything to do with my attempted abduction. Still, until we learned more, everyone was suspect.

THE SOUND OF LAUGHTER AND LOUD VOICES FOUND ME AS I made my way through the main hall into the kitchen area. The breakfast nook was crowded. Brielle and Anya sat on one side, with Rion sitting stoically on the other.

I was surprised to see all of them together, especially Rion. His rigid posture gave away his discomfort—a seemingly insignificant image that would forever be burned in my memory. He was so out of place amongst my friends, sticking out like a sore thumb, but I secretly loved it. Little things like this? They were the most important part if Rion was truly trying to gain my trust.

"Well, this is a surprise," I said, coming up and leaning against the island. I fought my smile as I looked at my husband. "I didn't know we were going to have company."

"Neither did I," he gritted, taking a sip of whiskey from the tumbler before him.

"I hardly got to see you earlier before you were swept away. I've been helping Anya with the dogs, and —" Brielle turned to Rion. "Anya said I had to ask you, but I was wondering if I could buy one of the pups when they're born and weaned..." she trailed, attempting, very poorly, to bat her eyelashes in his direction.

He stared at her. "Are you alright? It seems there is something wrong with your eye."

Anya and I looked at each other before laughing.

"No, I was trying to convince you to let me have one of your pups!"

"And that was how you chose to do it?" He grimaced. "You looked as though you were dying," he mumbled.

"Oh, put her out of her misery. Let her have one," I chastised before turning around and grabbing a wineglass from the countertop and pouring a drink.

Rion sighed. "Very well. They were meant to go to good homes, anyway."

"Really?" I asked, standing straighter. "Where do they go?"

"I run a charity for disabled children. Most cannot afford to own the service dogs they require, so I provide them."

I raised my brow, flicking my gaze to Anya. "You breed your dogs to go to children in need?"

"You look surprised, love. Yes and no. I do not typically breed them at all. In fact, the latest litter was a mistake. However, my animals are the best of the best and, as such, will make fine service animals."

I didn't know what to say. How could this man, this grumpy pain in my ass, be so empathetic underneath it all? It was difficult to reconcile who I was getting to know with the man I first met. They were completely different people.

"Sit," he said, patting the seat next to him. "Dinner will be here shortly."

While we waited, I chatted with Anya and Brielle about their plans for the rest of the week. Rion's arm rested along the back of my seat, his fingers occasionally brushing my shoulder. When my cousin brought up the mayor's gala, it reminded me to ask Rion about it. "Are we still going?"

He grimaced. "Unfortunately, yes. I tried to get out of attending, believe me. However, he will not listen to reason and has requested our presence."

I didn't have time to answer before three large pizzas were carried in by a familiar man, one who'd helped me many times. He was silent as he slid pieces of cheese pizza onto plates for each of us, disappearing once he was done.

"What's his name?" I asked Rion, taking a bite out of the delicious, cheesy food.

"That is Hendrix's son, Silas. He struggles with communication, but he is incredibly hard working and intelligent. I have tried to provide better employment many times, but he likes his station and chooses to stay in it."

"He's just shy," Anya said. "I've found him many times in the stables with the animals. I think he prefers their company to people."

Our conversation died down as we dug into our meal, often laughing or making friendly conversation. As we finished up, our bellies full of bread and cheese, I found myself resting my head on Rion's shoulder. He stiffened under the contact but relaxed as he intertwined our fingers under the table.

Silas came back in and quickly cleared the dishes. I

could barely thank him before he hurried out of the room faster than he came in. Brielle stood up and stretched, staring out the window at the inky darkness that had stolen the day.

"Stay," I said, reading her mind. Brielle hated the dark, and she hated being alone in it even more. Even when it came to driving. I wondered if that had anything to do with the restrictions on the fae, but there seemed to be something bigger to it.

I realized I hadn't asked Rion if it was okay, which isn't something I should have to do, but if he was going to work at whatever this was, then so would I. "Would that be okay?"

The corner of his mouth ticked up in a gentle smile at my question. "I suppose it can be arranged."

Brielle smiled. "Girls night, it is!" She pulled me up and into a hug. As she stepped away, I noticed Rion watching us intently. When his gaze met mine, I mouthed the words, "Thank you." He only dipped his head in acknowledgement.

Much to my surprise, Anya was unaccustomed to the rituals of a girl's night. Brielle and I were happy to educate her on the time honored rituals of self-care and gossip. After dinner, we went up to my bedroom. Brielle lit the candles, filling the space with the scents of eucalyptus, lavender, and sage, before raiding my cabinets in search of face masks.

It was mid-morning when we woke up in a tangle of limbs. Brielle's head was down by my feet while Anya lay near the middle of the bed, spread out as far as she could go. I felt the exhaustion wearing me down, but this was the first time since marrying Rion that I'd felt unmistakably happy.

In a strange way, I was thankful for the abduction. Without it, I don't know if things would have changed.

twenty-two

Brielle decided to stay until the night of the gala, much to Rion's chagrin, and I welcomed her company. The estate felt isolating, especially as I stared at the cityscape on the other side of the Odesza. It was bustling, full of creatures living their life to the fullest. Once upon a time, I would've counted myself amongst them.

I struggled to be the perfect daughter, seeking praise and adoration from a man incapable of giving them. But now that I was no longer under his wing, I didn't know who I was or what I wanted out of life. The possibilities were endless, and that was a terrifying prospect. Perhaps I'd talk to Rion about volunteering at one of his charities or even one of my aunt's.

Brielle had insisted on helping to style my hair, knowing I was helpless with such things. She had pinned the right side back with a diamond hairpiece, leaving it in loose curls flowing down my back. I teared up when she produced a pair of matching earrings, completing the look and making me feel elegant despite my nerves. "He's going to lose his shit when he sees you," she said, spraying my hair.

I looked back in the mirror, admiring the blush creeping across my cheeks. "Do you think so?"

"Absolutely! You look stunning, babe." Brielle reached for her purse, tossing her phone inside. Then she held out her hand. "You ready?"

I nodded and took her hand. As we rounded the corner and descended the stairs, my attention caught on Rion waiting in the middle of the foyer. He'd been talking to Hendrix when he turned, noticing our presence. His dark eyes sparked with silver, coming alive as he observed us. Hendrix clapped him on the back, leaning in to whisper something in Rion's ear.

He didn't move as we approached, sliding his hand into his pocket. "You look beautiful," he breathed.

"I could say the same about you," I said, circling him quickly. It *might* have been an excuse to check him out, but who could blame me? His tuxedo was perfectly pressed and tailored. "You clean up quite nicely."

He flashed a small smile and offered his elbow. "Shall we?"

THE TRIP TO THE CITY WAS QUICK. OUR LIMO APPROACHED a sleek, black skyscraper in less than half an hour. Photographers were already stationed outside, awaiting a glimpse at the mayor's guest list for the evening. Seeing them brought back the uncomfortable memories of leaving the hospital, the way they shouted those awful rumors at me.

As if reading my mind, Rion grasped my hand and pressed a kiss to the back of it. "I will be right by your side. As will Brielle." I stared at him only for a moment before I felt the truth of his words settle over me.

Those rumors were false, Calia. They didn't mean anything. They. Weren't. True.

She nodded in confirmation as Hendrix we pulled through the glittering glass awning. Security greeted us, opening the door and pushing back the small crowd that had formed. I kept my head down, allowing Rion to pull me to his side.

I wasn't sure why trepidation coiled through my body, fraying my nerves and setting me on edge. Nothing had happened, nothing had triggered me, yet still it lingered.

"You're safe, love," Rion whispered in my ear as we stepped through the lobby doors, heading straight to the elevator.

I stayed quiet. Despite my husband's words, I didn't feel safe. Not in the slightest.

The ride to the penthouse was painfully silent. Not even Brielle said a word as we were ushered into a lavish foyer. Everything about this place screamed unreasonable wealth. A glass staircase led to the third floor, where a giant chandelier was suspended from the vaulted ceiling. The interior design was a strange mix of clean, modern lines and old-world opulence.

Up here, we were amongst the stars. I was so close I thought I could touch them.

A surprising number of people milled back and forth, filling the space while soft music filtered into the area. "I thought we were going to be early?" Brielle asked, looking around.

"We were supposed to be," Rion said, taking a step away. "But it seems plans have changed, and we were not made aware."

"There they are!" a deep voice boomed. "I was beginning to think you wouldn't make it."

We turned to find the mayor walking toward us with a glass of champagne. He was nearly as tall as Rion, and the dark grey suit jacket he wore unbuttoned emphasized his broad shoulders. His salt and pepper hair was swept back, giving me a glimpse of a small lipstick stain on the collar of his shirt.

Classy.

Rion stepped forward and shook the man's hand before turning to me. "Allow me to introduce my wife, Calia." I shook his hand, recoiling at the slickness of his palm. "Calia, this is Mr. Graves."

"Please, call me Von. Mr. Graves makes me feel like such an old man." He threw his arm around Rion and pulled him close. Brielle and I looked at each other and cringed.

This was going to be a long night.

We followed the two of them through the throng of people as the mayor chatted Rion's ear off. To his credit, Rion tried his best not to look annoyed, but the stiffness in his shoulders and pursed lips told me everything. The roar of the crowd was too loud. Everywhere we went, I noticed the way people stared. Some even pointed in our direction.

"Everyone is staring," I whispered to Brielle. Insecurity reared its ugly head with each second that passed. I knew they were gossiping about the rumors of Rion's infidelity. No matter how hard he tried to keep it from me, I saw the news. The posts on social media were the worst, as some had taken the time to manipulate photos to push their fucked-up narrative. I only knew they were false because I'd seen the original pictures, and half the time, their technological skills were severely lacking.

"Don't pay them any mind. They just want to gossip. And until you prove them otherwise, they will likely believe the rumors in the papers."

"How am I supposed to prove my relationship?"

Brielle shrugged. "You're the one in love. Figure it out."

"I am not in love," I hissed. There was no way. *Absolutely not.* How could I love someone I barely knew? One who hadn't allowed me the opportunity to get to know the man underneath the mask?

Brielle didn't respond, only rolling her eyes before the mayor clinked his glass and captured our attention.

"Dinner will be served shortly. Why don't you all make your way to the dining room?"

One by one, people filed in and took their seats. The large dining table took up most of the space, undoubtedly brought in for the occasion. Waiters came around, pouring cocktails and wine as hors d'oeuvres were carried out on ostentatious silver trays. My aunt and uncle entered, their faces grim. My father, I noted, was nowhere to be seen.

Brielle stood and waved to her parents, pointing at the empty chairs in front of us. As they took their seats, my uncle grabbed his glass of whiskey and shot it back before signaling for another. My aunt looked at him from the corner of her eye, lips down-turned.

Rion's uncle took the seat beside us. His stare lingered on me far too long for my liking, but I straightened my back and paid him no mind.

We made pleasant conversation through dinner, most of which was interrupted by Von, who spent most of the meal boasting of his accomplishments. I already couldn't stand the man, and every word he uttered only worked to solidify that opinion.

"Tell me, darling," Von purred from the head of the table. "What is it you saw in this brute? He's positively dull." His laugh quickly died when he found me staring back at him.

"I think the better question is what he saw in me; Rion has much to offer."

Von laughed. "Oh, we all know what he saw in you."

His remark caused others nearby to laugh, the

lustful gazes of a few of the men lingering on my skin like spilt oil. Rion let loose a low growl as he squeezed my thigh in both warning and comfort. "You're too kind," I gritted out, gripping my fork tightly.

As dinner ended, the women began filtering out toward the living room. My aunt paused, waiting near her seat. "Come, Calia. Let's leave the men to discuss their plans of world-domination." Most of the men laughed, too charmed by her beauty to see the remark for what it was: a mockery of their self-opinion.

I remained seated, instead looking at Rion. "What about you?"

His jaw ticked. "I must stay here and take care of some business, Calia. You should go with your aunt and cousin." His tone was brusque, a startling change from how he'd been all evening. But it was a reminder that no matter how much he said he would try to quell my fears, his image, it seemed, still came first. Rion stood, buttoning his tuxedo jacket and holding out his hand. I stared at it momentarily, contemplating telling him that I didn't want to go anywhere in this penthouse without him.

"Come now, Calia. I do not have all night," Rion chided. Renwick and Von laughed from behind him, not attempting to hide their amusement at Rion's callous remark. I shook my head in disgust as I took his hand and stood. He tried to pull me close, but his eyes narrowed as I held firm where I was. After three tense breaths, he relented and dropped my arm. "Do not go anywhere alone. I will be back shortly."

I met his dark gaze and nodded once before pulling my lips up in a polite smile and looking around him to the mayor. "Goodnight, Von. Thank you for having us, in case I don't get a chance to see you again before we leave."

"You are always welcome here, darling. Preferably without your husband."

twenty-three

I stared at the woman before me, who'd been prattling on for fifteen minutes about the horrors of wearing her emeralds and not her diamonds for tonight's event. My aunt sat beside me, reaching for a bottle of wine and filling our glasses to the brim. She gave me a look that said we'd need it.

It'd been nearly an hour since I'd seen Rion or my uncle, which was beginning to bother me. When I'd asked my aunt about it, she said she hadn't the faintest idea where they had gone to. They'd never stayed long enough at these parties for my uncle to merit such an invitation.

Though the penthouse was spacious, it shouldn't be challenging to find upwards of thirty men sitting around a room, doing whatever they did when their wives weren't around. And I'd had enough of waiting for something to happen.

"I'm going to use the bathroom," I told my aunt, standing from the loveseat we'd commandeered.

She looked up. "Do you want me to come with you?"

I remembered Rion's warning to stay with either her or Brielle, but I didn't think my aunt would take kindly to my snooping. It would be easier if it was just me, anyway. "No, that's okay. I won't be long."

I started up the stairs, looking up at the skylight installed above. The night was dull, the light of the stars stolen by those of the city. I decided that was my favorite part of living across the Odesza on Rion's viridian isle. It was far enough from the man-made splendor that the gods' work could shine.

As I reached the second floor, I heard the unmistakable sound of a woman moaning coming from above. The third floor acted as an open space balcony. From there, you could see directly down and into most of the living area.

It was decorated differently than the rest of the penthouse. It was dark and sultry; the walls were a deep red with black velvet drapes over the windows. Leather chairs were scattered throughout, with half-smoked cigars still burning in the ashtrays. On the back wall was a single door. Gold filigree was inlaid in the black wood, surrounding the heavy knocker in the middle.

Three men sat around a woman, watching intently as she pleasured herself for their enjoyment. She worked her hips in time with her hand, and even I was entranced by her performance. My eyes scanned her body, meeting her heated gaze. She shook her head subtly, the men too locked in on the spot where her fingers were disappearing to notice.

Still, I approached the door with caution, reaching for the handle. To my surprise, it wasn't locked. Thick smoke filled the air, casting the room in a hazy fog. The lights above were low, barely bright enough to guide my way without running into objects.

The space opened, and I was greeted with a similar setup as outside. Except here, naked women were dancing on small, elevated stages while others were draped along the men's laps. Knowing most of these patrons, if not all, had wives downstairs made me sick.

Had Rion known it would be like this? Is that why he hadn't wanted me to come?

I tried to turn around and leave when someone caught my arm. I was jerked into a rigid body, the smell of rancid breath crowding the space between our bodies. Von stared down at me with a wicked smile. "Well, well, well... What do we have here?" He leaned in, running his nose along the shell of my ear. "You couldn't stay away, could you?"

"Oops," I said, feigning ignorance. "You know, I was looking for the bathroom. This is so embarrassing. I should be going now."

I pulled at my arm, but Von tightened his grip. "You aren't going anywhere, darling."

Again, I attempted to pull free. "Let. Me. Go."

"Perhaps you should have listened to your husband's advice and not gone anywhere alone." This man was a predator. He liked the thrill of the chase, and bedding the wife of a man like Rion would be the ultimate thrill. "But you're a bad girl, aren't you, darling? You like messing around so you can be punished."

I felt like vomiting, which wouldn't have been the worst. Especially if I ended up losing my dinner all over his expensive tuxedo.

He jerked me through a throng of people as I attempted to peel his fingers off my forearm. I scanned the room, trying to find Rion among the group, but I couldn't see him.

Von pushed me to the center of the room. "We've been given a gift, men," he said, eyes glittering. His words were met with excited mumbles by the men, their gazes ferociously hungry.

"You don't want to do this," I warned. "Your life will be forfeit the moment you touch me. I'll see to it myself."

Most of them laughed, while a few seemed to think better of participating in whatever Von had planned, and walked away. Still, there was no sign of Rion, and I was utterly alone in a room full of men who looked as though they would gladly kill me for their enjoyment.

Von stepped forward and ran a sweaty finger down my cheek. "Rion D'Arcy can't do shit to me. No one can. This is my house, and these are my rules. I'm afraid you've wandered into territory you can't talk your way out of."

He attempted to grab the back of my neck, but I

ducked. My fist connected with his stomach, and I felt a rush of adrenaline as his breath left his lungs. "You bitch," he wheezed. I didn't stay around to find out what else he had to say, pushing through the crowd. I felt the caress of their hands, the way they groped at my body senselessly.

Gods, gods, gods, I was stupid. Why did I leave my aunt? Why didn't I listen when I was told to stay put?

"Grab her!" Von snarled from behind. I almost reached the door when someone reached my waist and jerked me backward.

I cried out when a hand clamped over my mouth. I bit down on its fingers, kicking and hitting their arms. They cursed, but gripped me tighter. "Stop struggling," a voice commanded.

As my body went limp, I had the fleeting realization there would be no getting out of there unscathed. "What is this magic?" I asked as they laid me down on the top of a table. There was no need to bind my wrists or ankles; no matter what I tried, I could not move.

Von laughed. "I'm surprised you do not know the gifts that vampyres possess, Mrs. D'Arcy. You are, after all, married to one of the most powerful. I would imagine his compulsion would put Finnick's to shame."

Compulsion? I hadn't known that was real. My father cautioned me as a child, but most of the things he'd taught me about vampyres were little more than myths to scare young kids into behaving. From what I recalled, compulsion ensured vampyres could ask anything of anyone and receive it. They could order someone to do the worst things imaginable, and there would be no choice but to obey.

Von's hand drifted across my chest, and I screamed, praying to the gods for a miracle. "I swear I will kill you myself if Rion doesn't do it before I can get my hands on you, you sick bastard."

He clicked his tongue against his teeth. "You have such a mouth on you. I bet your husband loves that," he said, placing his thumb against my lip. I bit it hard, drawing blood.

The mayor grasped my throat, squeezing hard so I couldn't breathe. I tried to break the spell, but my limbs felt like they were held down by immense weight. No matter what I did, I couldn't move. "It's interesting, isn't it? I've heard things about Rion D'Arcy, rumors one might say, about how he lost his ability to love long ago. But you seem to be proving them wrong."

The door burst open, letting in a stream of muted light. I could make out the silhouette of two figures before chaos descended. "Get your fucking hands off my wife."

Rion.

I choked back a sob of relief as I saw his face. Men fled the room, unable to escape Rion'sradius of terror quickly enough. Some made it—those who had shown no interest in using me for entertainment. The door clicked shut behind them as soon as the last man was out. Rion removed his jacket and rolled his shirt sleeves to the elbow before leaping toward his nearest victim. His fangs lengthened, nearly gleaming in the low light as he bit into the man's neck and ripped his head from his body before turning toward another and plunging his hand through their chest. Both bodies dropped, landing in pools of their own blood.

My uncle stepped into view, brandishing a silver pistol. He pointed it at the vampyre Von had called Finnick. "Is this your handiwork?"

Finnick swallowed, unable to respond before my uncle put a bullet in his head. As soon as the vampyre hit the floor, I felt the weight of his compulsion lift, and I scrambled off the table. My uncle hugged me tight, and I closed my eyes against the thought of what could have happened. If they'd been only a moment later... But I couldn't think like that.

As I peeked around my uncle's arm, I saw Rion's shirt splattered in blood. Bodies lay littered at his feet, his breath coming in hard, ragged pants. He hadn't even used a weapon, choosing to decimate these men with his bare hands.

Von was the only man still living. He'd curled himself into the corner of the room, where the stench of piss increased as we got closer.

Rion hadn't looked at me since he'd seen I was safe with my uncle. I wasn't sure if he was avoiding my reaction to the carnage he had wrought, or if he was so furious he physically couldn't.

He stared down at Von, who was mumbling prayers to himself. "Please, please, please," he begged. "I didn't mean anything by it. Nothing was going to happen. It was a joke!"

Rion's hand whipped out and caught Von by the throat, lifting him from the ground. "Would you like to do the honors, love?" he asked, offering the mayor's body to me.

My uncle gripped me tighter. "No," he said, shaking his head. "Do not dirty her hands, especially not after what he did to her."

"She can decide for herself." My husband finally looked at me, and my chest ached from the force of it. His eyes were wholly silver, shining with malice and the promise of retribution. But he had ceded his revenge to me, so I could be the reaper of this pitiful man's life if I so desired.

I held out my hand for my uncle's gun. "No," he said once more. "No, I will do this for you if you feel it must be done, but I cannot let you feel the weight of taking a life."

"This man would have raped me. He would have passed me around to each person in this room so they could have their fill. And when they were done, he would have delivered me back to Rion's doorstep, or your doorstep, broken and beaten." My anger rose at the injustice of it all. How many times had this happened before? How many other women had he abused, defiled, and gotten away with it? "I will gladly be his end. I understand exactly how it feels to be helpless in a room with men who look at you and see only one thing."

My uncle looked at me with tears in his eyes, but

placed the weapon in my waiting palm. Even if he didn't want that burden for me, he understood.

I didn't hesitate, walking toward the man cowering on the floor. He cried relentlessly, but I felt no mercy. Instead, a lethal calm washed over me as I raised the gun to his head and fired a single shot.

twenty-four

I'd thrown up all over Von's body as soon as I'd pulled the trigger.

Rion called a crew to clean up the bodies before he and my uncle broke down the door. Within fifteen minutes, they'd removed the remains and disposed of them. I didn't ask any questions because, frankly, I didn't want to know.

The stench of blood was overwhelming. It coated every surface, seeping into the fabric of my gown. I looked down and scowled. "Why do you ruin my dress every time we go out?"

He shrugged. "Perhaps this one would not have been ruined if you had listened to me."

Well, he wasn't wrong.

He placed his hand on my back, guiding me out of the room and into the open space where my uncle and aunt spoke in hushed tones. They quieted as we approached.

My aunt threw her arms around me. "My darling girl," she said, pulling back and cupping my face. "Are you alright?"

I nodded. "I'm fine now. Just a bit shocked."

No one ever expects to be in a situation like that. Still, the evil of the world has a way of touching everyone and everything, eventually. It could have been worse, and I knew that. Respected it, even.

"What happened to the other women who were here?" I asked, turning to Rion.

"Most were homeless. Von undoubtedly trapped them with the offer of a better life, only to take it back once they signed their contracts to be in his employ. We ensured they were taken to one of your aunt's shelters so they would be safe. It is a temporary fix until we can find something more concrete."

My heart clenched at his words. It was difficult to rationalize the killer I'd seen half an hour ago, with the man who helped children obtain service dogs and sheltered women in need. But as each layer was revealed, I wanted to learn more. No matter how terrible or frightening it might have been.

"We should get home," he said, draping his tuxedo jacket over my shoulders.

We said goodbye to my family and left the building. Hendrix was already waiting outside with the limo.

Rion sat on the opposite side of me and began loosening his collar roughly. His hands trembled with barely contained anger, reaching for a bottle of whiskey which rested in ice between us. He uncapped the bottle and took a large sip, stretching the silence between us.

"Let me explain—" I began, but he held up a hand to stop me.

"I asked you to do one thing," he said, his voice carefully controlled. "One *fucking* thing, Calia, and you could not do it."

I pulled his jacket tighter around my body, searching for warmth and finding none. "It'd been a long time, and I was worried. I didn't know what you were doing, who you were with—"

"Regardless of the situation, I can handle myself. You, however, could not. You walked into their den without knowing what to expect, and you were nearly raped!" He leaned closer, nostrils flaring. For a moment, I saw a glimpse of the monster hiding beneath his skin. "Do you know what I would have done if that had happened? Do you realize the damage it would have created?"

"No," I said, dropping my gaze to my lap.

He gripped my chin and tilted it up, meeting his glowing eyes. "I would have destroyed *everything*. I would have ripped the world apart and even then, it would not have been enough to temper my need for revenge because you would still be gone."

"Why?" I couldn't stop the question because I didn't understand what this was between us. How had we gone from such indifference to whatever this was in such a short time? The most confusing aspect was that it felt right, like this was how we were always supposed to be. I hated that more than anything because it made me feel dependent on him in a dangerous way.

To my surprise, Rion whispered, "I do not know. I only know that I can no longer imagine a world where you do not exist."

I leaned into his touch as his hand slid to my cheek. His thumb brushed along my cheekbone, pulling me into a kiss different from all the others. Those had been born out of lust, a maddening need for one another we couldn't stifle. But this was softer. *Sweeter*. It was a promise we hadn't yet voiced, binding our two souls as one. It was a subtle longing for which there was no cure.

It was something born of... *love*.

The thought was fleeting, but it was there all the same. I didn't love him, did I? No, it was far too soon. But maybe this was what falling felt like—an absolutely maddening sensation of not knowing which way was up or if my feet were on the ground.

No, it couldn't be. I wouldn't let it be. Not yet, anyway.

Rion deepened the kiss, opening my mouth with his tongue. My toes curled at his gentle caress, causing heat to pool low in my belly. I wanted him, needed him, couldn't live without knowing what it felt like for him to own me any longer.

I pulled back, brushing my nose against his. "Take me to your bed tonight," I whispered.

His gaze softened, sweeping over my face as if memorizing every line. "I would not have let you go even if you asked me to," he said.

The limo stopped, and Hendrix's voice came over a speaker. "We have arrived, Mr. D'Arcy."

Rion reached over and pushed a button. "Thank you, Hendrix."

I pulled his jacket tighter before the door opened and stepped out. The adrenaline from earlier was fading, and coldness began seeping in to remind me of what I'd done.

You killed a man, the voice whispered. *You put a bullet in his head and killed him in his home.*

No, I thought forcibly. I did what I could to protect others from ending up in the same position. Men like Von would never stop once they had tasted such a lifestyle.

"Are you okay?" Rion asked, brows furrowing.

I nodded, not trusting myself to speak. He'd given me the choice, and I'd made it. But if he knew of my guilt, he would take the brunt of it, and something told me he had enough of it on his shoulders.

twenty-five

R ion and I walked through the foyer and up the stairs, stopping at the threshold. "It has been a long time since I've shared this space with anyone," he murmured softly. He cupped my cheek, running his thumb across the bottom of my lip. He dropped his gaze to watch as I sucked the tip into my mouth.

Without warning, he bent down and scooped me into his arms. My legs went around his waist on instinct, and I leaned forward to taste the salt of his skin. At first touch, he slowly climbed the second set of stairs, placing teasing kisses along my neck and chest before he pushed open the door and deposited me inside his room.

It was everything I imagined it would be. Dark, earthy tones, leather, and mahogany wood. Gold accents adorned an ornate mirror that sat above his dresser, where I saw him watching me with caution. Outside, the moon was already taking on a reddish hue, signaling the beginning of the blood cycle. A large, round window looked over the Odesza.

"What is it?" he asked.

"All these years, I would look up at this window and wish to know what secrets it held." I met his gaze. "It was you."

He stared down at me, and for the first time this evening, I couldn't tell what he was thinking. I reached up, smoothing the lines between his brows. "What's on your mind, husband?"

"You," he whispered just before kissing my lips.

"What about me?"

He paused, pushing my hair out of my eyes. "How I wish I could live in this moment forever, but I cannot." His gaze slid to the window behind me, looking at the moon. I wanted to know why he thought that, but I didn't want to ask. Not yet, at least. Because I selfishly needed to allow myself this pleasure, to know what it would feel like to let my guard down, even if only for one evening.

We could go back to whatever we were supposed to be tomorrow. But tonight, I wanted to indulge in the fantasy he promised, and not think of the pain I'd endure when he tossed me away.

"We may not be able to make it last forever, but we can enjoy it while we can," I said, taking his hand and leading him to the bed. "Come on."

Rion followed without question, allowing me to

push him onto the bed. There was no light except for that filtering through the window. Half his face was masked in shadows, yet his eyes still glowed. "Where are you going?" he asked as I stepped back and let his jacket fall to the ground.

I smiled. "Your patience will be rewarded, dear husband." Reaching behind me, I found the clasp of my dress and let it fall to the ground, revealing the lace lingerie I'd worn. It was a last-minute decision I found myself grateful for as he devoured my body hungrily.

His tongue darted to wet his parted lips as I slowly approached him. He reached for me, but I swatted his hands away as I dropped to my knees. "Calia," he breathed.

"Yes, husband?" I asked, looking up at him with innocent eyes, my lashes fluttering as I blinked slowly.

He groaned and fell back on the bed, covering his eyes with the crook of his arm. "You are too cruel to me, Calia."

I fumbled with his pants, finally loosening his belt and tugging the zipper down before reaching in to grip his hard length. "I'm not a tease if I follow through."

I pulled his cock free and rose on my knees to kiss the tip, relishing his sharp intake of breath. He fisted the sheets, restraining himself so I could explore his body without interruption. He was heavy in my hands, even more so in my mouth as I opened to take him.

"Fuck," he gritted through clenched teeth as I drug my tongue from the base of his shaft to the tip. He moved his arm, and I met his gaze as he peered down at me with hooded lids. Without breaking contact, I slowly slid him into my mouth until I nearly gagged. "*Fuck,* baby... If you keep that up, I will come down your pretty little throat too soon."

The endearment sent shivers down my spine, and I preened at his praise. I wanted more. I wanted to satisfy him, to make him crave my touch as I had craved his. I wanted to be his *undoing.* My tongue gently caressed his cock, exploring every curve and vein as I took him deeper until I knew what made him cry out and curse. I savored each slow, languid movement I made before speeding up and taking him down again and again.

Suddenly, he sat up and wound his fingers through the strands of my hair, jerking my head back. A thin line of saliva trailed from my lips, and he bent to lick it away. "Are you trying to torture me?"

"Maybe," I said, smirking.

"Then maybe I should do the same." With one hand still gripping my hair, he forced me to watch as he fisted his cock with the other. "Is this what you want, love?"

"Yes," I said, watching each slow move he made. Precum dripped from the tip, leaking down his aching shaft. He let his head fall back in pleasure as he worked himself, pulling my hair tighter until small tears rolled down my cheeks, and I couldn't help but whine.

"What does my needy little wife want? Does she ache for my cock?"

"Rion..." My voice broke as he released a breathy moan. I reached out and licked the base of his shaft, running my tongue along the spot where it met his balls. If he wouldn't let me have him, then I would take it.

He growled. "Beg for it, Calia. Tell me how much you need me."

"Please," I breathed, out of my mind with how badly I desired him. He could tell me to walk off this tower, and I would do it. "I have never needed anyone more than I need you right now."

He let go of my hair and placed his hand around my throat, pulling me to my feet and bending me over the bed. His hands roamed my body, tenderly caressing every inch of me. "What are these?" he asked, running his fingers along my thighs.

Shame washed over me. "T—They're scars," I mumbled into the bedding.

"From what?" he asked, barely masking the rage beneath the surface.

"Rion, this isn't the time—"

I yelped as he slapped his hand across my ass. "Tell me what these are from, or I will not let you come tonight."

It wasn't something I liked to think about. What started as a self-soothing tactic as a child turned into compulsive skin-picking as I grew up. It happened without thinking about it. Sometimes, I wouldn't know until I found blood coating my fingertips. And then, when scabs formed over the wounds, I would pick at them further until eventually my legs were littered with small scars.

"It's an anxious habit I picked up as a child," I said. I

was embarrassed by my dermatillomania, and wanted nothing more than to hide in baggy clothing. But then I felt the gentle trail of his lips down one leg before switching to the other. His tongue swept out over each scar, carefully laving each one with attention before moving to the next. "W—what're you doing?"

"If you cannot love yourself, I will do it for you until you realize how worthy you truly are."

I fought back tears as he worked his way back up my body and peeled my panties down, exposing me to him. "Oh baby, you are so wet. You are making a mess of yourself." His fingers swiped through my center before pressing his lips to my clit and biting down. The sounds I made were inhuman. Garbled words and sounds left my mouth as he coaxed pleasure from my body.

His fingers dug into my thighs, tugging me closer until there was no possible way he could breathe. "If I die with my tongue in your pretty cunt, I will consider my life well spent," he moaned against my flesh. I wasn't sure how he always did that, how he seemed to know what I was thinking before I said it, but I didn't care as long as he kept doing what he was doing with his tongue.

When he pulled away, he flipped me onto my back and kissed me. His lips glistened with my arousal, and I tasted myself on his tongue while clawing at the buttons on his shirt. "You are addictive," he said, kissing down my neck and trailing his mouth along my collarbone.

I groaned, too out of my mind for this man to think

straight. I wanted to admire his body as he had admired mine. It was only fair. "Get this fucking shirt off now."

"You are quite demanding, love," he said, smirking down at me as he undid the buttons one by one.

"Now, who's the tease?" I muttered, rolling my eyes.

He dropped it to the floor behind him, kicked his pants off, and ran his hand across my soft belly. Everywhere his fingers lingered, it set my skin aflame in a way I'd never felt. He gripped my hips and pushed me further into the soft mattress, lining up his cock with my entrance.

My breathing hitched as I felt his thick head prod against my center. Gods, there would be no going back after this—no way we could pretend things between us weren't changing. Did I want that? Did he?

I did. I wanted it so much that I could barely stand it. I wanted to be wanted by him, desired by him. And most of all? I wanted to be his undoing, the thing he thought about every minute of every day until I consumed him in every way possible.

He bent forward as if reading my mind and captured my lips in a soft kiss. "Say the word, love. Say the word, and I'll walk away. Because you're right—there is no going back after this. I will covet you, a treasure above all treasures."

Fuuuuuuck. This man knew what to say and do, making me melt in his beautiful hands. I glanced down where his cock stood proud, leaking and needy for my body. Rising on my elbows for a better view, I caught his lip between my teeth before whispering into the space between us. "Destroy me."

Rion let out a feral growl and pushed inside of me. I cried out, dropping my head back in ecstasy before looking back to where we were connected. His cock was so thick, so big. I relished in the ways he stretched me. Every muscle in his body grew taut as he fought to keep control.

"Do I feel good, husband?" I whispered. He nipped my neck and groaned before slamming home. I screamed out, wrapping my legs around him and keeping him fully seated inside me. This was home. This was heaven. This was hell. I'd never felt so full, and yet I yearned for more.

"Oh," he growled. "You have no *fucking* idea how good it feels to finally have your sweet little cunt grip my cock. It is like you were made for me."

"I was," I panted as he slowly retreated. "You and I are destiny. The gods, the curse, our fate—all brought us here." I lifted my hips and used my legs to pull him deeper once more. "So this pussy was made for you, just like your cock was for me."

Those words snapped something inside of him, causing his eyes to go wholly silver. I wasn't sure what caused me to say them, but they came to my mind without hesitation, and I voiced them without fear. Maybe it was okay to let myself explore this connection, to allow my heart to open up to the possibility of *more.*

He gripped the back of my thighs and pushed them forward, nearly bending me in half. As he drove in this time, the sensation was overwhelming. My eyes rolled back as he hit that elusive, special spot. I felt every ridge and vein of his cock as it throbbed with each relentless thrust. I clawed at his back with my hands, crying for more until only garbled noises left my mouth.

"Fuck, fuck, *fuck*," he chanted, staring down at me with the gaze of a natural predator. I didn't want to come yet, but my control was slipping. I didn't know how long I could last, especially with how he looked at me. As if sensing it, he smirked and placed his thumb over my clit, stroking it gently. It was just a tease, but it was enough to make me groan. "Does this needy cunt want to come?"

His taunting words only kindled the fire inside my belly. He pressed down on my clit, stroking faster and faster but never reaching the speed I needed. "Gods-dammit, Rion."

A sharp slap against my aching center had me crying out. I didn't have time to breathe before his hand came up and squeezed the sides of my throat, forcing me to look at him. Swirls of inky shadows and pure light danced with one another in his eyes. "Beg me to come." He tightened his grip. "Use your wicked fucking tongue I love so much, and beg."

I didn't have time to dissect the meaning of his words because I was too lost in the pleasure he allowed me to taste. "Please," I murmured, gasping as he withdrew to the hilt and slammed back in. His eyes were trained on the spot we were joined. "You should be the one begging." His gaze widened in surprise, but the corner of his mouth ticked up. "Use this pussy to make yourself come, husband."

He dropped his head and moved his hand to my clit, working in tight circles. I was mindless with need, standing at the precipice of the highest mountain, when I saw his own resolve cracking. Rion pounded into me until my vision darkened, and all I could focus on was the sound of our bodies slapping against one another. I cried out, feeling my body clench around him as I jumped from the cliff and dove deep into a sea of pleasure. There was nothing else but him and I.He hit a spot that sent my body careening into uncharted waters. Wetness gushed from between my thighs as he continued to piston his hips. My nails dug into his skin as I screamed, my legs shaking around his waist.

With one final thrust, he let loose a deep growl before flooding my body with his release. I felt each ripple of his orgasm shudder through him as he continued to slowly move inside of me. He caught my mouth in a kiss before whispering, "Look at the mess we made."

Rion pulled out of me with care, the mixture of our releases coating his cock, and laid next to me. I wasn't sure what possessed me to move, but I gripped him in my hand and stared at him before lowering my mouth to his softening erection. The taste of both our come wasn't something I thought I'd enjoy, but I did. It was intoxicating.

His fingers wound in my hair before pulling me up to his mouth. He kissed me slowly, allowing his tongue to seek access with a gentle caress. When he was done, he held me close to his chest. We laid together in the silence, listening to each other's labored breaths.

Sated, I studied the room. A tall bookcase stood in the corner next to a well-worn leather chair with a pair of reading glasses resting on the arm. My gaze caught on them, curious as to why he had glasses at all. Vampyres had exceptional sight. "They were my father's," he said, as if reading my thoughts. His fingers trailed in idle patterns on my skin. "He had an accident when he was young that damaged his eyesight. He could get around fine in his day-to-day life without them, but he was an avid reader and found the text too small."

He missed his father as I missed my mother. There was nothing we could do to quell that ache, either. It would live within us forever. That was the shitty thing about grief. It could hit you at any time and without warning.

"I feel closer to him when I have them near. As if he is still with me somehow." His voice was small, as though he'd never been allowed to admit that out loud until now.

"Oh, Rion," I said, turning to him and wrapping my arms around him. "He is. He always will be." I placed my hand on his chest. "Even if you can't see him."

Seconds, minutes, maybe even hours passed before I spoke again. "Have you ever loved anyone?" I startled myself with the question, especially as I tried to convince myself I *wasn't* falling for him. Because that would be insane. It would be absolutely out of the question.

Right?

Rion was silent for a long moment before he finally met my gaze. "Once. Long ago."

I was surprised he'd answered, but I wanted to know more if he would allow it. "What happened?"

Another beat of silence. "She was murdered."

Oh gods. I hated asking, but I found my fascination with the matter interesting. There wasn't a single part of me that was jealous, either. His history spanned further than mine, and it would've been foolish to assume he'd never been touched by the potent fervor of love. Instead, I mourned for my husband and the love he'd lost. The pain he tried to hide was written in the night sky of his eyes, forever frozen as a constellation amongst the stars of his memory. A single tear fell down his cheek, which neither of us moved to wipe away. That wasn't how pain worked. You couldn't simply wipe the slate clean and start over. It lingered.

I reached out, running my fingertip softly across the soft, raised skin of his scar. His muscles tensed under my touch, and he watched me curiously before clearing his throat. "Have you?"

"Never," I answered without hesitation. Nor had I ever felt an inkling of the feeling.

Until possibly now.

But I couldn't tell him that. Now, it was more important than ever to keep my heart guarded as best I could because I could see Rion D'Arcy shattering that never and turning it into an always.

twenty-six

I fell asleep in his arms after our conversation died down. We hadn't spoken much after I'd asked him about his past, and I was okay with that. Great, even. The seemingly tiny grain of truth he'd given me had been one more thing I hadn't known before. And that, I decided, was progress.

My hand reached out, searching for him in the dim morning light, but he wasn't in bed. I blinked away the haze of sleep before pulling the sheets around my breasts and sitting up. He sat quietly in his armchair, tracing the outline of his father's glasses as he stared out at the Odesza. It was such a light, reverent movement—a careful caress that resembled longing. A book was in his lap, but he paid it no mind.

Though I knew he would hear me, I was quiet as I gathered the sheets around my body and left the bed. The wooden floor was cold against my feet. He looked

257

up as I approached, a tender smile gracing his face. "Good morning," he whispered, reaching out for me. Rion pulled my body to him, circling his arms around my soft waist. For a moment, neither of us said anything as we watched the water below crash against the rocks.

These were the moments when I forgot about our past, the curse, his family, and my own—all the things that ultimately would have led to our unhappiness or doom. Gods, it still could. If his mother or uncle found out about what happened, they would be less than enthusiastic. And it wasn't about the sex; I was sure they wouldn't care about that, but it was what the moment meant that threatened to be our doom.

And if I was honest with myself, which I hated, I knew the dynamic between Rion and me had been in a state of constant evolution since the moment we laid eyes on each other. I didn't know where it would take us, and even though I was scared as hell, a part of me wanted to find out.

The other wanted me to run as far away as possible because the depth of emotion this man could stir inside my chest was dangerous.

What did I really have to lose, though? We were forced to be together for the rest of our lives, or we would face the wrath of the curse and die painful deaths. But even a horrific death would not compare to the embarrassment and pain of his rejection if he decided he no longer wanted me.

His arms tightened around me as his lips grazed my bare shoulder. He peppered the skin with delicate kisses, sending those stupid butterflies fluttering in my stomach. It really was unnatural how my body reacted to his actions.

"How did you sleep?" he asked, resting his cheek against me.

"Very well, after someone drove me to exhaustion," I said, turning to look at him. His eyes danced with delight, the stars in them sparkling mischievously. Gods, he was breathtaking.

"Is that so?" he murmured, leaning in. "Perhaps you need to be exhausted once more..."

I squealed as he took me in his arms. Before I could blink, he laid me gently on the bed and removed the sheet dress I'd created. He placed open-mouthed kisses along my chest, taking special care as he worshiped each breast with gentle adoration. Already, I felt my body growing malleable under his touch.

"You're insatiable," I panted as he sucked my hardened nipple into his mouth. His tongue swirled around the sensitive tip, and I couldn't help the small whimper I let out.

"I crave those little noises, love. The ones you make when you are trying to stifle your pleasure." His hand slid down to my center without warning, and he groaned. "You are dripping for me..."

I could do nothing but nod my head as he slowly slipped two fingers inside me and climbed down my body. Sex with him was unlike anything I'd experienced before. It was dirty, raw, and passionate. I wanted to die from the pleasure he provided

Rion's fingers gently curved up, massaging the spot that had my back arching off the bed and my nails digging into his back. I could still feel the raised skin from where I'd marked him last night. "Right there," I panted. He didn't stop, increasing the pressure until my orgasm peaked, and I screamed his name. He lapped at my release, growling with each soft mewl that left my mouth.

Rion moved up, pressing kisses along my thighs, soft tummy, and breasts until finally landing on my mouth. As I moved to return the favor, he shook his head and stopped my hand from gripping him. I quirked my brow in confusion.

Did he not want me to touch him? Had I been bad at it?

Oh gods. If I was, I'd never been told so before. Somehow, disappointing him would be worse than any other.

No, don't be stupid, Calia. Don't let those insecurities in.

"It is not because I do not want you to bring me to my knees, *literally*," he said, smirking down at me. "But I believe your uncle is currently pulling up to our home, and I would rather not keep him waiting."

I fought a wicked grin. *Our home.* The two words set flight to another pair of fluttering wings inside my chest. "What if I promise to make it quick?" I asked, moving to my knees and kissing down his bare chest.

He watched me intently as I took his cock in my hand and stroked it with increasing pressure. I teased the crown with my tongue and finally understood what he'd meant about the sounds of pleasure being such a turn-on. Every single one he made had my pussy soaked, aching for him to fill me as he had done last night. But I also wanted my mouth to be the reason he lost control. The thought had me taking him down until I gagged.

"Fuck, baby. *Fuck*," he hissed. "You are taking my cock so well." His fingers wound in my hair. "But you have been such a naughty girl, sucking me down while your uncle walks inside our home."

The obscenity of his words had me craving more. He'd lit a fire inside of me I thought would never burn again. And I didn't care who saw me on my knees for him because I was lost to whatever spell this man had cast on me. He could have brought an audience in, and I would still let him do what he wanted to my body.

His grip tightened as he lifted his hips and began fucking my mouth. Saliva dripped down his shaft as I choked, holding back tears. Rion didn't relent, though. If anything, it only drove him to a point of no return. "I am about to come down that tight fucking throat," he grunted, looking down at me with a sense of adoration and lust. "Is that what you want?"

There was no chance to answer as his release filled my mouth. I swallowed greedily, licking his length for every last drop. He fell back against the bed with a sated smile before motioning me forward. I crawled over his body, feeling his hands skim across my naked flesh. "Sated, husband?"

"Not when it comes to you, wife." He smirked and

pulled me in for a chaste kiss. "Now, you really must get dressed because your uncle is causing a fuss downstairs with Hendrix, and I do not want to kill your family so early on in our marriage."

I pushed off the bed and sauntered toward his closet. My clothes were in a heap on the floor, and I had no desire to ever allow the fabric of that dress to touch me again. Rion looked at me for a long moment before walking behind me and ushering me into an enormous closet. I had *never* seen one so large.

"Is that right?" I asked, looking around at the shelves of nearly identical shoes and the hundreds of ties neatly rolled away behind clear glass. Overpriced suits and dress shirts lined the walls, pressed and ready for him to wear.

He gripped my chin, bringing my focus back to him. "We have an eternity together, wife. I am sure a little murder between our families is inevitable."

I swatted his hand away, pondering his words. "It sounds as though you're already planning it."

"Not at all. However, history has a way of repeating itself... You are a Darrow, and I am a D'Arcy."

"No, I'm not," I said, crossing my arms.

He quirked a brow. "If memory serves me, and my memory is excellent, your name is Calia Darrow."

"It *was* Calia Darrow."

Rion smiled, finally catching my meaning. He stepped forward, cupping my jaw. "And what is it now, wife?"

"D'Arcy," I breathed, skating my lips across his. I

pulled back, watching the confused expression on his face. "You know, by Kallistos law and everything."

"You little shit," he said, laughing. He grabbed a shirt from the rack, drawing it tight between his hands before popping my ass with the fabric.

"Ow!" I cried, pressing a hand over the hurt. "What was that for?"

"Oh baby, that was nothing..." he purred, eyes gleaming with a predatory delight. "I am capable of so much more."

Rion surged forward, but I stopped him and placed my hands against his chest. Something was bothering me, and I knew this conversation wouldn't go well, but we needed it. "No, no, no! We need to talk about it before you hypnotize me with your dick again."

He chuckled. "Hypnotizing you with my—"

"Dick, yes. Now, we need to talk about Jasper."

His face fell, all traces of the playful, loving man I knew gone. "No." He dropped his shirt in my hands and proceeded to his bathroom, where he started the shower.

"You need to let him out, Rion. It wasn't his fault, it was mine."

He stepped under the stream and ran his hands through his hair. "Regardless, he knew there would be consequences for his actions. And you were still abducted, despite your foolish actions." His gaze dropped momentarily to the raised scar on my hand.

Gods, the man was impossible. He refused to see

reason. "Rion, this is insanity. If you don't let him out, then I will."

He narrowed his eyes. "You would not dare"

I met his stare. "Try me."

"Go meet your uncle, Calia," he said, pouring soap onto his sponge and dismissing me.

He was infuriating. How could he go from being such a wonderful partner to whatever this was in front of me? And in such a short time? I thought he wanted to work on our communication and openness, to earn my trust. But all he'd done in that time was give me mind-blowing orgasms and make me dick-drunk.

"You are such an ass," I muttered before turning on my heel and shrugging his shirt on. "This conversation isn't over."

"Yes, it is." His body pressed against mine, droplets of water seeping through the fabric separating us. The soft caress of his breath fanned over my neck as he moved my hair over my shoulder.

But I wouldn't let him sweet talk me into letting this go. Because if I let him do it now, he would expect it every time we disagreed. He would think he could bat those pretty fucking eyelashes and cast his stupid spell, and I would quite literally do anything he asked.

I turned and pushed him away. "Let him out, Rion. And don't treat me as one of your staff. I'm your fucking wife."

"Why do you want him out so badly?" he asked, crossing his arms over his massive chest.

"Because whether you want to admit it or not, we

need help figuring out what is going on and why someone is after me." I softened my gaze and took his hands in mine. "You trust him. I know you do. And I think we need to hold those people close during times like these."

Rion tilted his head to the sky and let out a sharp exhale. "I will see to it."

I quirked my brow. "Before lunch."

"Fine," he gritted out. "I will handle it immediately."

"Thank you, husband," I whispered, rising onto my toes and pressing a chaste kiss to his lips.

I SAT ACROSS FROM MY UNCLE IN THE KITCHEN WITH A CUP of coffee in my hands. He'd hardly said two words since we sat down. Once I'd left Rion's room, my uncle's gruff voice rang throughout the halls of the manor. He'd seen me sneaking back to my room in nothing but one of Rion's long dress shirts that barely covered my ass.

Needless to say, it was one of the most embarrassing moments of my life. It felt like a betrayal to my family that I enjoyed Rion's company. Actually, it was more than just enjoyment. It was becoming an obsession that had me chasing a high only he could give me.

Castor finally cleared his throat. "Are you well?"

"That's a bit of a loaded question," I said, lifting the cup to my lips and taking a sip. "Physically, I'm fine."

"And emotionally?" he asked, softening his gaze.

I sucked in a breath. "Well, that's the tricky part, isn't it?" Despite the reprieve being with Rion provided, it was hard not to remember the feeling of being utterly at someone else's mercy. The helpless feeling as Finnick cast his compulsion on me, and the way I was forced to feel their hands on my body while unable to stop it, had struck a new kind of fear in my heart.

Which was something I needed to discuss with Rion. What powers did he have, and what could I do to protect myself from the gifts of others? I felt so stupid for not knowing anything about his people other than what my family had told me. I shouldn't have relied on their biased descriptions and limited knowledge. This had been my destiny since the day I was born, so why hadn't I asked more questions or done more research?

But I didn't want to talk about last night. I didn't want to give that nightmare a chance to grow and fester in my mind. And while I really wanted to ask him about the symbol he bore on his body, and why it matched the one on every person who tried to kidnap me, I knew now wasn't the time. I forced a smile. "Anyway—" I sipped my coffee "—what're you doing here this early?"

"It is nearly noon, Calia," my uncle said in a deadpan.

"Still doesn't answer my question," I mumbled under my breath.

He reached out his hand to cover my own. "I wanted to check on you. That look in your eyes..." he trailed off, shaking his head. "I could not sleep thinking about what would have happened if—"

"Don't," I said, closing my eyes. "It didn't. End of story."

"Calia—"

I shoved up from the table and pushed every thought from my mind. I couldn't sit here and listen to this any longer, and I didn't want to sit by and do nothing, either. I fought the urge to pick at my skin, knowing it would only bring a vigorous round of guilt if I gave in. "Do you want to train today?"

My uncle blinked up at me, undoubtedly wanting to push the topic, but choosing not to for my sake. "Will that help?"

"Yes," I said without hesitation.

He stood and pressed a kiss to my temple. "Lead the way, little star."

twenty-seven

Sweat poured down my temple as I braced my hands on my knees. We were in Rion's private gym which boasted a fully furnished training ring. I hadn't known it existed until Silas showed us, keeping his head down and hardly speaking.

When I told my uncle I wanted to train, I hadn't expected him to quite literally kick my ass. He stared down at me with a wide grin. "Is that the best you can do, little star? I thought I taught you better."

I rolled my eyes and walked over to the small water fountain in the corner. "Yes, well, I have a feeling you were pulling your punches back then."

"Perhaps," he chuckled, before wiping the perspiration away from his forehead. His bare chest glistened, all his tattoos on display. They consisted of a mixture of strange symbols and connected lines. At first glance, you would think it an odd composition, but somehow, they blended as though they belonged. He noticed me staring at him and lifted his chin. "What is it?"

"I've always wondered what those meant," I said, pushing from the ground and nodding toward the marks. "They aren't from a language I recognize."

Castor looked down at the art marking his skin. "It is from our mother tongue—something that has not been spoken in a very long time."

"Why did you get them?" I asked as he gestured for a bottle of water, which I tossed to him. I needed to keep the conversation casual to get anything out of him. My uncle could spot deceit with little effort, especially if it was someone he knew. I couldn't count how many times he busted me when I was growing up.

"Remember, Calia, I am not from Kallistos. My people are warriors—it is in our blood. This tattoo was inked onto my skin when I was a child. It is a sign of my birthright, the duty to protect those who cannot protect themselves."

His narrowed eyes met mine, and I felt a strange current of energy run between us. What was that supposed to mean? That somehow that symbol was mixed up with the meaning of protection? I wanted to laugh. It was almost ironic, given how the group who'd attempted to kidnap me had borne the same sign. Protection was the last thing on their mind as they tried to rip me away from everyone I knew.

But symbols could change depending on who wielded them, and perhaps that was what the group attempted to do. Because the absolute last thing I wanted to believe was that my uncle was somehow mixed up in this mess.

"Why do you ask?"

Shit. He knew, and he knew that *I* knew. I couldn't tell him my fears, though. Because the dynamic between us would be forever changed if he was involved. He'd been the closest thing I had to a father–a real one, anyway.

Was that all a lie?

I shrugged, looking away. "I was just curious."

His stare was still boring into me, the weight heavy on my shoulders. "Has Rion found out any more information on your kidnappers?"

Double shit.

What would be the worst thing if I told him the truth? Or a semblance of it? I was in my own home, surrounded by the house staff, security, and my husband himself. Castor would be foolish to attempt anything here.

"Actually, he found a symbol that links them together," I said, pulling my hair back into a ponytail. I watched my uncle as I spoke, searching for any hint of recognition. "He isn't sure what it means, though Anya has found some old books of her father's that may help us."

"That's excellent news," he said, reaching for his shirt and throwing it on. Dread pooled in the pit of my stomach. I wasn't sure why I thought he was lying, but there was just something about how his words seemed to coat my skin in oil that left me feeling disgusted.

"There you are," Rion said, smiling as he walked through the glass door of the gym. He pressed a kiss to my temple before turning toward my uncle. "Thank you for agreeing to help with her protection."

My uncle turned to grab his gym bag and swing it over his shoulder. "Of course." He glanced at me. "I will see you in a few days, little star."

"Would you mind if I walked him out, love? There are a few things I would like to discuss." My gaze shifted between the two men, and I could only nod. I know I should tell Rion of my suspicions, but he would lose his fucking mind with no regard for the truth. It wouldn't matter if my uncle was involved or not; the accusation would be enough for him.

What I needed was proof.

THE NEXT FEW DAYS PASSED IN A BLUR.

While my uncle went out of town, something that only added to my suspicion when Rion told me, I'd taken the liberty of holing myself up in the massive library with Anya and Brielle most of the day. Anya brought in every book her father owned. They were currently spread out on the floor, the tables, and even a few armchairs. We spent our time bouncing around from book to book, jotting down any notes that could possibly help us.

The blood moon was quickly approaching. Rion's sister would be arriving by the end of the week, and the entire house was frantically preparing for the celebration. I'd never seen so many people in the halls since I'd been here. Anya said the bustling crowd was typical for a D'Arcy event, but more exciting, given the reason. She'd been little when the last one occurred, but she could still recall the thrum of magic permeating the air. Vampyres would dance under the red sky, their skin nearly aglow with power.

Brielle, on the other hand, told me how the event brought about concerns for the fae. The vampyres were at their strongest during the cycle, and we were at our weakest. Many of our kind refused to leave their houses, which made little sense to me, given we traditionally couldn't be in the same place at the same time unless it was under the safety of an enchantment.

Rion dragged me out of the library each night, taking me to his bed and fucking me until I couldn't move. There were moments I would catch him staring at me like he was scared our time together would end at any given moment. I felt the same way, constantly waiting for the rug to be swept from beneath my feet.

I'd never experienced anything close to love before. Still, with each moment I spent in Rion D'Arcy's arms, I felt that changing. Would I survive the fall if he let me go? I didn't think so.

Tonight, I stayed even later in the library than usual. Anya had gone home to Poppy, who was due any day now. She asked me to take a break and come with her, but the sun had already set by the time she left, and I was confined to the house.

My research into the symbol kept bringing me back to the days of the First King, Calix Darrow. My mother had named me in his honor because she claimed I was destined to lead us into an era of peace, just as he had. As my uncle had mentioned, it always came back to protection. Of what, I couldn't figure out.

But since I kept circling around my ancestors, I decided to go back through the matched couples over the centuries. After all, our curse started because of his deal with a sorceress. And maybe some of this research was due to my own curiosity about the history between the Darrow's and the D'Arcy's.

My father had kept my knowledge of our curse to a minimum. It was always something I accepted without question. But now I couldn't help but wonder why that was?

I hunched over the large leather-bound book in front of me. The smell of dust lingered in the air. From what I could tell, there'd been only six ceremonies throughout the past millennia. *Six*. The longest marriage had lasted nearly four hundred years until it ended in blood. Both had been found in their beds with their throats slit, clinging to each other as if they had a chance. After that, many of the matches ended in various states of bloodshed. Every case, except for the one, showed the deceased party as a Darrow.

But why? Why were they being murdered? The whole point of this curse was to force the families, and by extent, their factions, to coexist. So why weren't they lasting? And who was out to get them? Nausea churned as I thought about my kidnappers.

Was I next?

I reached out for my coffee mug, frowning as I noticed it had gone cold. Gods. How long had I been in here today? I hadn't left for lunch. Silas was kind enough to bring Anya and me sandwiches and sparkling water. Rion had left to meet with his uncle this evening in the city, and I didn't want to be in my room alone. We hadn't talked about where I would sleep if he wasn't home, which was silly when I thought about it. I was his wife; I should be sleeping in his bed. But something stopped me when I thought about trudging up to the tower alone.

I rubbed my temples, scanning down the text until I found the union before Rion and I. Hmm... That was strange. Despite it having been fairly recent, there was hardly anything written under the log. I re-read the entry again. Thick, black lines were drawn through their names. They almost resembled burn marks. The dates underneath were little help, only citing the date of their ceremony and the year of death.

My fingertips ran across the textured pages. Just as the others had been, a Darrow had died. My father and aunt were the only children my grandparents had, and I was an only sibling. If Brielle had a sister, wouldn't she have mentioned it? Especially if she died. So, who was this mystery woman?

"Still awake?"

I jerked up to see Jasper standing in the doorway, his hands behind his back. His eyes looked like hollow pits with tiny gold flecks in the dim lighting. While he looked better physically, I could tell he was far from being okay.

"Jasper!" I said, pushing away from the table. He smiled at me hesitantly, gesturing toward the seat in front of me. I nodded eagerly, watching his slow approach.

He stared at the numerous books littering every open space and raised his brow. "Doing a bit of light reading?"

I let out a humorless laugh. "Something like that," I said, running a hand through my hair. Exhaustion was wearing on me, and not just from the countless hours of research I'd done. Since the moment Rion D'Arcy entered my life, it'd been in an absolute whirlwind. There hadn't been time to breathe. If I wasn't fighting for his attention, I was fighting for my life.

I studied the man before me, noticing how his time away had affected him. "How are you?"

Jasper sucked in a sharp breath. "I am still settling in." The muscles in his throat worked as he stared at me. "Being away, like *that*, takes a massive toll on your body. And after tasting your blood..." he trailed off, shrugging.

Both of us stayed silent. I didn't know what to tell him. 'I'm sorry' didn't seem like enough, especially given his torture. "Jasper, I—"

He held up a hand to stop me. "Don't, Calia. What's done is done. And regardless of the consequences of my actions, you saved me. I would have died in that garage if you had not offered your blood. I regret not being quick enough to stop you from being abducted."

We both sat down at the table. Jasper pulled a small flask from his pocket, shaking it lightly before handing it over. "This conversation will likely require something a bit stronger."

The alcohol burned my throat as it went down, but a sense of calm washed over me as I slid it back to him. We were silent, neither wanting to bring back the memories of that terrible day but needing to all the same. "What happened after they took me?"

Jasper blew out a sharp breath. "When a vampyre feeds from a living being, it lulls our body into what we call the daze. It does not matter what's going on in the world around us. We are focused on taking in the sustenance we require or seeking the high of pleasure it provides. But it is almost impossible to snap out of it once we are in the daze. Thoughts and actions are fuzzy, nothing quite makes sense. It's as if—"

"As if you're in a daze?" I asked with a smirk. It amazed me how much I still had to learn about their kind, but I was an eager student.

He laughed. "No one said vampyres were original. Either way, I entered that mind space once I fed from you. When you were ripped away, I knew what was happening. I knew I should stop it, that I needed to get up and take you back, but my body refused to cooperate. Blood is the most intoxicating drug, and once its influence falls, there is no going back."

I didn't realize how much it affected them. My uncle had told me once that vampyres don't often feed directly from living beings because of the consequences that follow, but I didn't realize what they were until now. If done at the wrong time, it could mean your demise.

"When was the last time you fed from someone?"

Jasper thrummed his fingers along the table. "It's been years—decades, really. He worked here in the manor. I don't know how it began. We'd become good friends, but somewhere along the way, it grew into more."

"What happened?" I was almost afraid to ask, knowing this story wouldn't end happily.

He smiled sadly. "He grew sick. The kind that all the magic, potions, and power in the world could not have cured. I was there when he took his last breath."

I reached out on instinct and placed my hand atop his. "It sounds as though you really loved him."

"I did. Given the chance, I would have liked to live a life with him, I think. But our world is not always kind, and that dream is not always obtainable."

I recalled my conversation with Rion when he'd found Jasper and me in the kitchen. He'd said Jasper would toss me away after he used me, but now it made sense. The man in front of me was broken, searching for someone who would light a fire in his heart the way someone had once before.

"What was his name?" I asked softly, careful not to break his tender reverie.

"Finn," he said, tone melancholy before turning

toward me and clearing his throat. "Now, where can I help you? Rion said you've been held up here looking for information on a symbol?"

Quickly, I filled him in on what I'd learned so far—which was next to nothing—until we landed on what I was studying before he came in. "But look at this," I said, shoving the book of pairings toward him. "The information on the union before Rion and I is redacted. I can't find anything about it." He furrowed his brow, scanning the text. "Do you know anything about them? You were around then, right?"

He shook his head. "Rion and I were not in Kallistos, then. His father sent us both to school around that time."

Well, *shit*. I had hoped I could ask Rion about it later, but Jasper ruined that idea. I just didn't understand why their records were erased. Who were these two people, and who had something to hide by ensuring their identities never came out?

I could ask my aunt, but with how my uncle had been acting lately, my trust also wavered with her. It broke my heart, but I suddenly felt unsure about their constant love and affection over the years. That was crazy. Surely it hadn't all been a ruse.

The only people left were Rion's mother and uncle, both of whom terrified me to varying degrees. There was absolutely no way I could speak to them about this. They didn't even like me. No, scratch that. They loathed me. Half the time, they looked at me like I would become their next tasty meal.

I groaned in frustration, leaning back in my seat. Jasper rested his head on his palm while he studied me. "Why are you lingering over this? I thought you were researching some symbol."

"I was. I mean, I am." I paused before scrunching up my face. "I've been searching for days and can't find anything. I've looked through every old, dusty book I can find, scoured websites for old relic records, and you know what I have to show for it?" I threw my arms wide. "Nothing but more questions. But this? This feels important whether it pertains to that stupid symbol or not."

He leans forward over the table. "If these records were sealed, it is likely for a reason, Calia."

"My life is apparently at stake, Jasper. I'd say my curiosity is warranted," I snapped.

He raises his hands in surrender. "I said nothing about not helping you, but just warning that this may lead you down a path you cannot return from. You must be ready to accept information you may not be ready for."

"What's that supposed to mean?"

He sighs. "Calia, this woman is your ancestor. She was afflicted with the same curse placed on your shoulders, yet you have heard nothing about her. Doesn't that seem strange?"

Obviously, it did, or I wouldn't be holding onto this the way I was. "Of course, but—"

"So it stands to reason that someone is lying to you.

At the very least, they are keeping information from you, but why?"

Maybe because my uncle is involved with the people who want to kidnap and possibly kill me? This was all getting to be too much. Up until a couple of months ago, I was relatively normal. Nothing crazy happened to me. But now I found myself in a tangled web of secrets and danger that I couldn't unravel.

Jasper pushed up from the table. "Come on. It's late. There will be no solving this tonight. If it makes you feel better, I will see what I can find out."

"What makes you think you can get me information I can't get myself?" I asked, forcing my body to stand. Every muscle in my body ached. As much as I wanted to go to bed, I wanted to soak in a warm bath more.

"Will you just trust me?"

Famous. Last. Words.

twenty-eight

I woke up to the feeling of lips against my neck and the sharp scrape of fangs along my skin. My back arched off the bed as I wrapped my arms around Rion's muscular body, enjoying the tantalizing scent of fresh mint and whiskey. His body was seated between my thighs, allowing me to feel his cock thickening along my core.

Rion's calloused hands skated along my arms, pinning them above my head and interlocking our fingers as he ground into me slowly. *Deliciously.* His name left my mouth like a plea, and I finally opened my eyes to see him staring at me in wonder.

"Good morning, wife," he murmured, peppering kisses along my collarbone. "You were not in our room this morning."

Our room.

Guilt warred inside with my shame. When Jasper

and I left the library last night, I allowed my insecurities to get the better of me. Instead of heading up the tower to Rion's room, I solemnly made my way back to mine, where I fell into a restless sleep. I was still unsure of my feelings and frankly a bit terrified of the way he already captured my heart in such a short time.

"Allow me to put that pretty mind to rest," he said, pressing an open-mouthed kiss along my collarbone. "I want you in our bed every single night."

"How do you do that?" I asked. This wasn't the first time he'd seemingly read my mind. Each time he did it, something else quickly stole my attention. Well, not this time. No matter how tempting it was to let it slip.

He continued blazing a path across my chest. "I told you I could read people. It is one of my many talents."

I pulled away from his touch even though I craved it more than air. He really had a way of distracting me. "Reading people is a lot different than knowing their thoughts," I said, deadpan. "Whatever you do is something more."

"Perhaps it is." Rion peered down at me. "Does that bother you?"

It wasn't an admission, but it was *something*. "I don't know," I answered honestly. "Does that mean you can hear every thought that pops into my head?"

"I have learned over the years to tune people out. The mind is a deafening place. Even though they may not recognize it, a single person constantly thinks about a hundred different things at once. But you," he paused, tucking a strand of hair behind my ear. "I can single you out in a room full of thousands. Your thoughts always reach me like the chime of a crystal-clear bell, beckoning me home."

Oh gods, my heart was soaring. This was it. I *was* falling in love with him. No matter how much I tried to protect myself, I didn't know how long I could go on pretending. I'd wanted to take things slow, because why should we rush something we have our whole life to figure out, but to hell with that. He'd touched and nurtured a part of me I hadn't known needed tending, which now belonged solely to him. In fact, *every* part of me belonged to him.

Then, with a sickening realization, I remembered the conversation we just had. Heat flooded my cheeks. Judging by the smile on his face, he'd realized my blunder before I had.

I didn't know what to say, or if I should say anything, so I leaned in and kissed him gently instead. No words could adequately express the unfamiliar emotions I was experiencing. But where they failed, my actions would succeed.

Our tongues tangled as desperation increased. This man was everything. Rion had embedded himself in my skin, my blood, my very being. There was no going back. I knew what I wanted, and I wanted *him*. Even if an infinitesimal voice whispered for me to hold back, to not give him my all. I shoved that panicky feeling away. It had no place here.

His fingers dug into my skin roughly as he explored the expanse of my body. On a whim, I'd decided to sleep naked last night, something I never usually did but had gotten used to with Rion. He was fully dressed, still in his suit from last night, and somehow, it made the situation hotter.

He bit at my breasts, causing sharp twinges of pain and pleasure to coexist. "Those fucking noises," he growled, biting me harder. "Do you feel how hard they make me, Calia?"

Rion rotated his hips to prove his point, not that he needed to. Suddenly, he sat back on his heels and stared down at me. It would normally make me insecure, given every blemish, scar, and stretch mark was on display. But when I looked into Rion's eyes, I saw nothing but adoration. He slowly traced the soft parts of my tummy and thighs, and I fought the urge to flinch.

Insecurities aside, the voices of doubt had been brutally programmed into me from an early age. It was hard to repress those memories and how they made me feel, but somehow, he quelled my urge to run.

"*Beautiful*," he whispered, tracing a silvery scar curving along the plump side of my stomach. He leaned in and kissed me, softer this time. I still felt the pangs of desire we'd had moments before, but this was his way of showing me his feelings without having to voice them. Allowing ourselves to say it out loud made it too real, and no matter my feelings, I didn't want to force Rion's hand. We had our whole lives, our very long and immortal lives, for that to happen. Yet, with each caress of his lips, I knew one thing with absolute certainty.

Whether he voiced it or not, I knew Rion was falling

just as hard as I was. I only hoped we didn't crash and burn.

I pushed the jacket from his shoulders as he worked at the buttons on his shirt. We never took our eyes off one another, careful not to burst whatever bubble we'd found ourselves in. Dropping his clothes to the floor beside the bed, he rested in between my thighs once more and dragged the head of his cock through my center.

"You are already drenched," he mused, looking down at the wetness coating his length. "Look at the way you glisten, baby..."

I lifted onto my elbows, watching as he slowly sank into me fully and withdrew. His cock glistened with my arousal, even in the early morning light. He repeated the motion over and over, driving me wild with languid movements until I could take no more. "Please," I rasped.

Without warning, Rion thrust forward and took me in his arms. He rolled us over so I was straddling him. We groaned in unison at the change, the new angle he was hitting causing me to clench around his length. Even though I wanted to move, the two of us lingered in this moment just a little longer. His forehead came to rest on mine as his hands moved to cup my ass. "What have you done to me?" he whispered.

"The same thing you did to me," I whispered back, arching into his body. He buried his head in my neck as I began to move. His soft, muffled grunts caused goosebumps to spread across my skin, igniting a fire in my belly that knew no bounds.

He guided my hips, urging me to move faster until sweat dripped down our bodies. I didn't know where I ended, and he began. We were a mess, a tangle of limbs that I never wanted to unravel. The pleasure building could be my demise.

"*Calia... Calia... Calia...*" My name was a chant on his lips, a prayer from a man stranded in a drought. I was his rain. I was his salvation. I was his everything.

"I know, baby," I whispered, clinging to the moment with every fiber of my being. Whatever this feeling was between us was much more than we had bargained for. "I know."

"I want to own every part of you," he confessed. "I want to know what brings you pleasure. I want to know every thought running through your mind. I want—" But he stopped abruptly and shook his head, clearing it of whatever thought he was about to voice.

I cupped his face with my hand. "Tell me."

He grasped my wrist and pressed a kiss over my pulse. "I have been waging an internal battle with myself from the moment I saw that scar on your hand, knowing it was another man's mark gracing your body."

"Then mark me," I said without hesitation.

His finger traced the outline of Jasper's bite. "I do not want to hurt you—"

"You won't." With my words, there was a shift in the overwhelming emotions coursing through us. They offered a future both wanted but were too afraid to take.

But there was no going back for me. We were together, whether either of us wanted to be or not. The fact I felt as deeply as I did about him only cemented my decision. I leaned forward and captured his bottom lip between my teeth, causing his eyes to flash. I spoke slowly, drawing out the words, "Make me yours."

Rion wound his fingers through my hair and gently pulled my head back. His nose trailed along my throat and down to my chest. He stopped above my heart, taking the time to explore the spot with his tongue. His gaze shifted up in question, but I nodded my head.

I wanted this. I wanted *him*.

His long canines slowly elongated, teasing the tender skin of my breast before they pierced my skin. The sharp pain made me cry out, but not in pain. *In pleasure.* This euphoria transcended all others, for no mortal sensation could adequately explain this feeling.

His cock twitched inside me as I moved my hips, eagerly seeking pressure against my clit to accompany the heat coursing through my being. This was better than any high, any drug. It was a tantalizing blend of ecstasy and vulnerability, allowing him to etch himself upon my flesh in the most permanent of ways.

I was lost to reckless abandon, and so was he. His glassy eyes grew feral as he threw me down on the bed without breaking us apart and hammered his hips home. Crimson rivulets streamed down my breast as his pace increased. I slipped my fingers between us and circled my clit, crying out in relief as a wave of pleasure rolled through my body.

"Come," he growled, pulling away from my skin. Blood dripped from his mouth onto my skin. "Come for me."

As he dropped his mouth back to the bite, my body shattered with the force of a deadly storm. It raged and raged within me, causing my body to convulse as his body slammed into mine. Our garbled curses became one as we rode out the waves he created.

He let out a guttural cry with one final thrust as his hot release filled me. Slowly, the bliss abated, and we fell back against the sheets, sharing a moment that felt more intimate in its simplicity. His tongue licked the wound, sampling the co mingling of my sweat-slicked and blood-stained flesh. Remnants stained his lips, and without thinking, I leaned in and kissed him.

The copper tang was foreign on my tongue, but not unwelcome. His eyes dropped to my mouth as we pulled apart, his gaze growing glassy. As he laid back down, he tucked me close to his chest and stroked my bare back. There were no words to explain what we'd just experienced, so we held on to each other until our breathing slowed, and we slipped into sleep's embrace.

A LOUD BANGING ON THE DOOR HAD RION AND ME bolting upright in bed. I didn't know how long we were out, but my mind was foggy as though waking from a trance. His hair was sticking up in a million directions, something so utterly mundane, yet my heart constricted all the same. "Wha—" I began before stopping abruptly as a female's voice sounded from the other side.

"Rion D'Arcy! Get your ass out here!" I turned to him, raising my brow. If this was Senna or any of his other groupies, I would personally cut off his dick and throw it in the Odesza. He winced at my thoughts, but pushed off the bed and padded toward the door.

What the fuck? Was he seriously going to answer that? My sheets were bloodied and disheveled, a flashing sign above our bed to anyone who walked in about what we'd done.

"I swear to all the fucking gods, Rion—"

Her voice was cut off as he ripped open the door. The woman launched at him, wrapping her arms around his neck and squealing. He looked at me over her shoulder as he embraced her.

I'd never considered myself the murderous type, but right now, I was seeing red, and it took every ounce of strength I had to not sink my nails into her skin and pull out her pretty little throat.

"Gods, Cal," Jasper muttered, walking in behind the woman and sitting on my couch. "Bit much, don't you think?" I opened my mouth to answer him before he pointed in my direction. "Nice tits, by the way."

I gasped, scrambling to pull the bloody sheets to my chest as though they could save me from whatever weird situation this was turning into. Rion, ever the calm and collected one, dropped the woman. He picked up the nearest object and lobbed it at Jasper's head. "Shut your fucking mouth."

The woman ambled over to the couch beside Jasper and dropped down. "Way to go, asshole. Now you've gotten him riled up."

I put two fingers in my mouth and whistled, drawing each of their attention. "Okay. What the *fuck* is going on? Who are you?" I asked, pointing at the petite woman in my room. She had long, soft blonde hair and golden-brown eyes. Her skin was so pale it almost had a pink hue.

She looked over to Rion, pouting. "You haven't told her who I am?"

He pinched the bridge of his nose. "I have not had the time."

"Then what have you been doing? You've been married for—"

"I have been busy. I know you do not understand the concept—"

Her eyes nearly bugged out of her head. "What's that supposed to mean?"

"It means that while you have been off gallivanting—"

Jasper watched with a gleeful expression as the two volleyed insults back and forth, while I couldn't understand what was happening. "Hey!" I screamed above the noise. Three pairs of eyes swiveled to me. "Someone explain this," I said, waving my hands in front of me.

The blonde popped up and pushed past Rion until

she stood before me. "Since neither of these dickheads will introduce us, I will." She held out her hand. "I'm Rowena. Rion's sister."

twenty-nine

Oh, thank fuck. This was Rion's sister, and suddenly, I felt like an idiot for assuming it was yet another one of his admirers. When I looked closer, I saw the similarities between them. The slight upturn of the tip of their noses and high cheekbones. The fullness of their cupid's bows, marking their lips in a natural pout. But that was where it ended, because the rest of Rowena's looks belonged to their mother.

Thankfully, she didn't seem to have the downright bitchy attitude to match.

"Oh, I like her," Rowena purred, winking at her brother. "She doesn't mince her words."

"I am well aware," Rion said, crossing his arms. Sarcasm dripped from his words, but his eyes softened as he looked between his sister and I.

I inwardly groaned. "Can all vampyres read minds?

Or am I just unlucky to live with the ones who can?" I'd spent so many moments falling over Rion in my thoughts while acting as though I wasn't affected on the outside. The smug uptick of his lips told me just how much he'd enjoyed that.

"Hasn't my brother explained anything to you?" she asked incredulously, plopping herself at the end of my bed. "These special traits, gifts, powers—whatever you want to call them—are inherited from bloodlines. So while we can hear your thoughts, we can't shift like others can."

"Shift?" I asked, raising my brow.

Rowena shrugged. "Yeah. All nocturnal animals, you know, for obvious reasons. I had a friend who could transform into a cat once. I would sneak her in when my mom was being a cu—"

Jasper's laughter rang out as Rion scolded his sister. When Rion turned to his friend, Jasper didn't look the least bit sorry. "What? She is."

Rion closed his eyes and tipped his head to the sky. "By all the gods..."

I stared at the three of them dropping into casual conversation, repeatedly ending in Rion muttering under his breath. For the first time, I was allowed an uncensored look into the company my husband kept. He seemed to love these two fiercely, even if his patience sometimes got the better of him. Which, given Rowena's boundless energy, made sense. But they were family, and no matter how much they bickered, their eyes lit up being in the same room as one another.

Rowena pushed off the bed and grabbed Jasper by the arm. "Enough being rude. We obviously interrupted something." Her eyes flitted briefly to the spot on my chest, which had become visible in my relaxed state. He mumbled about Rion owing him for entertaining his sister, but something told me he didn't mind as he followed her out.

When Rion and I were alone, he stepped between my legs and gently pulled the sheet away from my chest. His fingers reverently dusted his mark before meeting my eyes. "Does it make me a monster if I want to see these litter every inch of your skin?"

I shook my head. "No, because I wish I could do the same."

He smiled. "Are you getting territorial, wife?"

"When it comes to you," I said, gripping his neck and pulling him closer, "always."

RION AND I BOUNDED DOWN THE STEPS OF THE MASSIVE staircase hand-in-hand. We were freshly showered, though it'd taken us nearly an hour once we stepped underneath the hot water. He was insatiable, pounding me against the tile wall while sinking his teeth into my shoulder. After, he rode out the remainder of his daze while I dusted the towel across his body and combed his hair.

I liked the way he let me take care of him. It showed

a new vulnerability and level of trust to both of us. We both had one loving parent who was taken too soon, while the other had made it their mission to make our lives a living hell. It was fitting that we were destined for one another.

We were lost souls adrift, searching for someone to understand, finding it in the most unlikely places.

Leonora and Renwick stood in the middle of the foyer, speaking in hushed tones before they turned and saw us. Their gazes drifted to where Rion's fingers were intertwined with mine.

His mother's sharp lips curved into a smile that had my stomach dropping. "How nice of you two to finally join us. Especially as the preparations are already in place for the festivities this evening."

Rion pulled me closer to his body. "Thankfully, you handled it, Mother. Just as you always do."

His uncle scoffed. "As the future head of this family, boy, you should have been by her side to oversee this." His eyes flicked to me, screwing up his nose in disgust. "But it is obvious where your priorities lie."

"My priority is my wife, as it should be." His fingers flexed on my hip, biting into my skin.

"Well," I said, attempting to turn the conversation around. "We are here now. Is there anything we can do to help?"

Raised voices had us turning around in time to see Enyo bound through the back door with Anya on his heels. "Come here, you little shit!" she called, her face turning red as she noticed us watching her.

The massive dog skidded to a stop before me, tongue lolling out the side of his mouth. I bent forward and scratched behind his ears. "Hello, handsome," I cooed. "Are you being a handful for Anya?"

The woman in question caught up with a huff and clipped a leash to Enyo's collar. "Sorry about that," she said sheepishly, avoiding Leonora's malicious glare. "We were training outside when he took off running toward the house."

"Get that nasty thing out of this house," his mother hissed, pointing a sharp finger toward Enyo. He didn't seem to like that much, though, as his hackles raised, and he let out a low growl, his eyes shifting to pure black in a warning.

I snapped my fingers and ran my hand over the dog's head, claiming his attention. "Enyo," I commanded, and to my surprise, he turned his haunting gaze to me before sitting back on his haunches. Anya apologized profusely, shooting a grateful look my way before ushering Enyo out of the house.

Leonora crossed her arms. "I do not know why you still have those beasts, Rion. They are nothing but a nuisance."

"I have them because they protect those important to me and are loyal. Something I am sure you would not understand, Mother."

"Watch your fucking mouth, boy," his uncle growled.

His mother didn't seem offended by his words. In fact, she appeared utterly unfazed, as though this kind of talk was typical between them. It shouldn't have been a surprise, given what Jasper had told me about their relationship. But my heart ached for the man whose mother showed him no love.

Her gaze drifted over my body, stopping her perusal at my neck. "What is that?" she hissed, looking between Rion and I.

My hand drifted up, brushing against the mark against my shoulder that Rion had left this morning. I thought my sweater would cover it, but it must have slipped just enough for her keen stare to notice.

"What?" Renwick asked, stepping forward quickly and jerking my hand away to uncover the bite.

Rion's hand shot out and gripped his uncle's wrist. "Get your hands off my fucking wife," he snarled, nostrils flaring.

"You cannot be serious," Renwick shot back. "You have claimed her?"

"Yes," he said through gritted teeth. "And if you want to keep your hand attached to your body, I suggest never laying a finger on her again."

The two men stared at each other, primal power filling the air until I nearly choked on the tension. I didn't understand what the problem was. Maybe it was just old prejudices at work. It wasn't a secret that neither liked me or thought me suitable, but at some point, his mother had wanted Rion to woo me. Now that he had, what was her problem with it?

"Rion, can I speak with you for a moment?" his mother asked, clearing her throat.

"No."

"Rion—"

"I said no," he snapped, finally shifting his gaze to her.

I placed my hand on his arm. "It's okay. I should head to the library, anyway."

"Then I will come with you." Without a word, he nudged me toward the library, leaving his mother and uncle in the foyer. Neither of us spoke as we walked the short distance, and no matter how much I wanted to break the silence, I didn't know what to say. I could never understand their family dynamic; maybe it wasn't my place to.

As soon as the door clicked behind us, Rion dragged me to him. His hands cupped my cheek, kissing me with a desperation I felt throughout my entire body. He moved us backward until I bumped into the table. "Let's go somewhere tonight. Just you and me. Fuck this cele- bration. Fuck my family. Fuck that stupid fucking moon," he muttered between kisses.

I pulled back. "What? No. This is important to your family—your people. You need to be here for them if nothing else."

"They are hardly family," he said with a harsh laugh. "Family does not treat each other as though they are dispensable. Family does not belittle each other. Family does not—"

I placed my hand against his cheek and pulled his haunted gaze to mine. "Leonora and Renwick aren't your family." He opened his mouth, but I placed my finger on his lips. "Let me speak. They are not your family—they are your blood. There's a huge difference between the two. But Jasper and Rowena? They *are* your family and likely want to celebrate the holiday with you."

A muscle flexed in his jaw. "I would rather get as far as possible from this fucking house."

"Why?" I questioned, grasping his clammy hand with mine. "What is so terrible about being here?"

The doors opened, and Jasper walked through, stopping as he saw us. "Should I have knocked?"

"Don't play stupid," I said, rolling my eyes. "Even I know you have exceptional hearing."

He shrugged one shoulder casually, draping his arm across the back of the couch as he sat down. "It was worth a shot."

Rion narrowed his eyes. "What are you doing here?"

"Calia enlisted my help with research," he said, tapping his foot. "She found some missing information regarding the union before you and believes it might be related to the symbol."

RIon turned to me, brows furrowed. "Why do you think that?"

I ran my hands through my hair to expel a sudden jittery sensation crawling along my skin. "Because every mention I found regarding that symbol goes back to Calix Darrow. So, I started looking into those affected by the curse." He stepped back and crossed his arms, listening intently. Having his undivided attention was nerve-wracking, but I was proud of what I'd found. "Each match has effectively signed a Darrow's death sentence, and it's been in the most horrible ways, too. But this last one... It was the shortest at only twenty-two years, and all information on it has been redacted."

"So?"

So? Was he serious? Surely, he could admit it wasn't normal. "That doesn't seem strange to you?"

A muscle in his jaw flexed. "No. It does not. With the evolving technology, they could have easily done so for privacy."

I waited for him to elaborate, but nothing came. I don't know why I was surprised because we always took one step forward and two steps back. "Privacy?" I barked out a laugh. "There is no privacy between our families. However, there is a history of my ancestors being slaughtered like cattle while yours kept their lives. Excuse me if I don't want to suffer the same fate."

"You won't," he said, gripping my face. Something like worry came over his face, but he fought to keep it neutral. "I swear by it. As fascinating as this must be, it has nothing to do with the symbol."

Irritation flared as I knocked his hands away. "How do you know, Rion? How do you know there is no connection if you refuse to entertain the idea?"

"Just drop it. Please."

"Just drop it?" I hissed, pushing from the table and stalking toward him. "You don't know any more than I do, and you don't get to diminish my fears. This affects *me.* My life. I thought that would be important to you, but maybe I was wrong."

His eyes blazed with reciprocated anger. "If you truly

believe me to be that heartless, then perhaps I should not bother to try and change your mind."

Jasper came up and stepped between us. In the heated exchange, I'd forgotten he was even here. And even through my frustration, I didn't really believe what I'd said. I knew he cared about me, but why the hell didn't he want me to pursue this lead? It may lead to nothing, but what if it didn't? What if it unmasked the assholes who tried to kill me?

Rion ran a hand along the back of his neck, blowing out a sharp breath. I didn't know what he was thinking, but his expression was fearful as I took a tentative step forward. "This is important to me," I whispered. "And I want it to be important to you, too."

Rowena opened the door, humming an upbeat tune as she removed her headphones. "Calia, it's time—" She stopped short, her gaze darting from person to person. "Oh, I'm sorry. I didn't mean to interrupt. Mother told me to take Calia to her room to get ready."

My gaze dipped to my feet. Suddenly, I didn't feel like celebrating anymore, especially when Rion refused to take my concerns seriously. And I sure as hell didn't want to sit in a room full of people who hated everything about me, my family, and what I represented. No matter what happened between Rion and me, they would never accept me.

The prejudice ran too deep.

But even though I hated that, I hated thinking about being alone with Rion more. Especially when he could apparently turn a blind eye to my fears so quickly.

Anything would have been better than that, even if he had to lie.

The weight of his stare was heavy as he approached. He already knew my thoughts. There was no point in wasting my breath. I closed my eyes as he pressed a kiss to my forehead. When I opened them, he was gone.

thirty

Rowena led me from the library, going on about what we would both wear tonight. The first night of the cycle was the biggest celebration. The vampyres powers would peak while inhibitions floated away on the wind. My mind fought to keep up with each kernel of information she let slip, but it was useless.

I was a million miles away, standing at the edge of a cliff, wondering how I got here. There was a chance Rion was right; maybe the matches had nothing to do with me, and this was simply a fixation my brain conjured to make me feel as though I was doing something.

But what if it wasn't? What if this group had been targeting the Darrow lineage because of the mistakes of our ancestors? Fae and vampyre alike often hated the restrictions binding them to their celestial body. But I didn't know what they stood to gain by our death. There was no way to break the curse. Many had tried before to no avail, wasting their lives for a cure that didn't exist.

I looked into the mirror above my dresser, wiping away the errant tear falling down my cheek. I didn't want to be next. I didn't want to be another life taken by people who wanted to use me.

The sun was setting on the horizon, and soon, night would fall. I could see the outline of the blood-red moon hanging high in the sky, a beacon for the vampyres to emerge, claiming the night as their own. Unease landed on my shoulders, and I wished I'd taken Rion up on his offer to leave. Gods, why didn't I? Because now all I felt was apprehension creep into my mind as each second ticked by. The danger of the evening was imminent, and the acrid taste of fear filled my mouth.

"I made this for you," Rowena said, pulling out two massive garment bags from my closet. She unzipped the one with my name on it, revealing the most beautiful dress I'd ever seen. It was so much sexier than I'd generally go for, but the thought of Rion ripping it off me gave those butterflies of desire a reason to flutter.

"Okay, gross," Rowena mumbled before stripping me bare and shoving me into the contraption. The corseted top consisted of little more than black lace, with a plunging neckline that dropped to my navel. The skirt was full, with a slit that came to mid-thigh, baring my right leg. My breasts were pushed so far up that they were the first thing I could see when I looked down. Both bite marks were on full display. I touched the raised skin, feeling a tingle brought on by the soul-deep possession it represented.

I was his. He was mine. Now, it was time for the whole world to know it.

"And I thought we'd pair it with this," Rowena said, grabbing my attention by dropping a small box into my hands.

I opened the lid and pulled out the gift, eyeing it closely. "Do you think this is necessary? I mean, it's beautiful, don't get me wrong, but isn't it inviting trouble?"

She smiled conspiratorially before taking it from my hands and fastening it in place. "I think you're about to walk into a room full of people who hate you--"

"Well, that was rude."

"And I think you should show them why you are the wife of Rion D'Arcy. Why the curse chose *you* to stand at his side." She stepped back, eyeing her handy work with pride, then let out a little squeal. "It is perfect!"

The sound of a string quartet striking up in the foyer floated to us, signaling the first guests' arrival. Rowena pushed me down in front of the mirror, running her hands through my copper strands as she thought. "Now, what are we going to do with this hair?"

THE PARTY WAS IN FULL SWING BY THE TIME WE descended the stairs. She'd braided my hair into a coronet, weaving in strands of metallic red fabric through the plaits. Paired with dark smokey eyes and blood-red lips, I barely recognized myself. For once, I looked like I belonged in this room. Even though I knew any confidence I exuded would come crashing down as I tried to avoid the eyes of curious onlookers.

Rowena grabbed two flutes of champagne as a waiter passed by and handed one to me, which I took eagerly. It would take a lot more alcohol to fake my way through this evening, but it was a start. Rion was nowhere in sight, and I hadn't heard a whisper since our heated moment in the library earlier. We'd even waited for him in my room, Rowena stating he should be there to escort us down. But five minutes turned into ten, which turned into thirty, and we couldn't wait any longer.

"It'll be fine," Rowena murmured. "I know it seems like a lot right now, and it can be really overwhelming, but—"

"But just smile and wave?"

"Exactly," she said, grabbing two more drinks as we discarded our first. "Remember that there isn't a person here who isn't trying to impress someone else. It's all about putting on a show and hoping for the best."

"What about you? Who are you trying to impress?"

"Oh," she said with a laugh. "I'm the exception to the rule. I have everything I could ever want outside these walls, and Rion keeps our mother off my back so I can keep my freedom."

I grinned. "That sounds pretty amazing."

She brought her glass to her lips. "It can be. It's also very lonely."

I was about to ask her more when Jasper approached the two of us with outstretched hands. "Damn," he said, whistling. "You both are visions." His eyes slid down my thigh, where Rowena had fastened the leather knife holster she'd gifted me earlier. Inside was a small dagger with a ruby-red blade. "Expecting trouble?"

Rowena turned and raised an eyebrow. "What'd I tell you? Everyone is kissing ass tonight."

I laughed, my heart jumping as I scanned the room behind Jasper for my husband. When I didn't find him, an ache settled within my chest. I reached up and traced the raised scar over my heart. Jasper tracked the movement, and I quickly moved my fingers to my necklace. "Where's Rion?" I asked, trying to keep the nerves out of my voice.

Jasper took a sip of his whiskey. "Ah, he'll be down shortly. Renwick is currently holding him hostage in his office."

Before I could ask more, Rowena grabbed my hand and dragged me into a lavish ballroom. I'd never been in here before, which was surprising because this room was massive, taking up a substantial portion of the estate. The ceilings seemed to extend to the heavens, a swirling mirage of stars fluttering above our heads. I looked up in awe, realizing this was the closest I'd been to the night sky. I took in a deep breath, swearing I could taste the chilly autumn air on my tongue.

"Rion said you were always staring out the window at night," she said, smiling up at me. "So he wanted to bring the stars to you."

Tears sprang to my eyes, threatening to demolish the masterpiece Rowena had worked so hard to create. Jasper came up and placed a hand on my back in comfort as we all looked up at the twinkling lights dancing above to their own beat.

"Enough of that," Rowena said, thumb swiping beneath my lashes. "Let's dance."

She spun me around in circles, laughing until we cried as time passed in a blur. Jasper would occasionally jump in, even though he had absolutely no rhythm. There was a euphoric high in the air, and for the first time this evening, I let myself be free from the burden of my thoughts. My mind had wandered far enough, and there would be time for more tomorrow, but I wanted to live for today.

The three of us made our way to the bar, ordering an assortment of drinks because we couldn't decide. "Why not get them all?" Rowena and Jasper said in unison as they filled a tray with cocktails. I followed them to a small table in the corner where the crowd was in full view.

The atmosphere in here was wildly different than that in the foyer. This was wild and reckless, strobe lights incessantly filling the air with their white light as bodies writhed to the beat of the music. The other was still haunted by the sounds of string instruments, where old men sat around and smoked cigars while eye-fucking any woman who wasn't their wife. It was only then that I realized Rion still wasn't here.

I turned to Jasper. "Where is he?" I yelled over the music.

"Don't know!" he yelled back, finishing a shot of clear liquor that Rowena shoved into his hand.

Movement caught my eye as Senna walked through the door in a floor-length black satin gown that hugged her body as though painted on. Her hair fell down her back in perfect waves, not a single hair out of place. "Fuck," Jasper muttered under his breath before reaching over and tapping Rowena on the shoulder.

Her eyes grew wide, a snarl building in her throat as Senna stopped in front of our table. "Well, well, well..." she purred, taking the time to scrutinize our appearances without saying a word. My hands dropped to the skirt of my gown, playing with the soft fabric to keep myself from slapping that stupid grin off her face. But her gaze stopped as she eyed the marks along my skin, her expression morphing into one of anger.

Jasper sat back, draping his arm around me. "And just when I thought this party would be free of snakes," he said, shaking his head. "The queen herself shows up."

She narrowed her eyes at Jasper. "And here I thought you might have thought up some better insults, but I suppose that is too much for your small brain to handle."

Jasper tipped his head back and laughed, only growing Senna's anger. He placed a hand over his heart in mock hurt. "Oh no, how will I ever go on?"

"What are you doing here, Senna?" Rowena asked, handing me a fresh drink. I silently thanked her for something else to occupy my hands.

"It's the blood moon, Rowena. Everyone is here," she said, gesturing toward the crowd.

"No. What are you doing *here*? As in our table? You know, where no one wants you?"

Behind me, Jasper high-fived Rowena. But it was Senna's next words that sent my heart plummeting. "I was talking to Rion moments ago and told him I was dying to see you." A wicked smirk crossed her lips. "But now that I've seen you, I should be returning to the party." She turned and sauntered through the crowd.

I watched her go as Jasper and Rowena whispered reassurances in my ear, but I couldn't shake the black cloud that now hung over my head.

I should follow her...

No, that would be stupid.

But isn't knowing the truth better than speculating?

"I need some fresh air," I called out, fleeing the room before Jasper or Rowena could stop me.

There was only one way to find out.

My heartbeat thundered in my ears, covering the music from the party as I made my way up the staircase. Somewhere in the sea of people, I'd lost track of Senna. It was okay, seeing as I didn't care what she did, as long as she stayed away from Rion. I didn't trust her and knew she would stop at nothing when digging her claws into my husband.

As I'd parted the crowd, I also noticed Renwick and

Leonora's absence. Seeing the way Leonora had micro-managed every aspect of the evening, I assumed she'd be taking full advantage of enjoying her hard work.

I stood at the bottom of the second set of stairs leading to Rion's bedroom and office. For the first time since I'd left the party, I'd hesitated. My hand rested on the thick mahogany railing, and I contemplated turning back. It was the smarter option of the two. I could spend the rest of the night dancing, drinking, and having fun. When Rion showed up, I would throw my arms around him and kiss him under the stars, tangling our tongues and limbs until we became one.

That's what I *should* do, but I didn't put much stock into following the rules.

More than anything, I just wanted to see him. This afternoon was stupid, and we'd both reacted poorly. I wanted to tell him that as I got down on my knees and asked for forgiveness with my tongue.

Raised voices drifted down, and my curiosity won out. I stepped slowly, though I knew the noise from below would help mask my footsteps. The door to his office was cracked, deja vu rushing over me. The first time I'd snuck up here, I'd seen and heard a similar sight. Unlike that time, however, it wasn't Leonora on the other side.

It was my uncle.

thirty-one

Rion sat behind his desk, his fingers steepled together as he stared at my uncle pacing before him. "What do you want, Castor? You have taken up more than enough of my time already, and I would like to get back to my wife."

My palms slickened with sweat as I waited for the answers to questions I didn't know if I even wanted. What the hell was my uncle doing here? And why was he standing in front of Rion, pacing back and forth like a caged animal readying to break free?

Somehow, amidst the chaos, I knew whatever I heard here would irrevocably change the course of my life.

As he turned, I saw his wide eyes and flared nostrils. He was pissed. And that was likely too flippant of a word to describe the look on his face. It was terrifying and cruel. "I didn't know who you were when I laid eyes on you in that church," he mumbled, wiping sweat from his brow. "But there's been a nagging sensation in my mind urging me to remember. It has kept me up most nights, and Vivian thought I was going mad, but then it struck me."

Rion's jaw hardened. "This conversation is over. You should leave before you no longer have the option," he said, nodding toward the door.

"I do not know how you've hidden your past so well, but your secrets end here." Castor was lost in his thoughts, and I was enraptured. Guilt told me I should leave, but curiosity begged me to stay.

"And what secrets are those? Please enlighten me."

Without hesitation, my uncle met my husband's silver glare. "When will you tell her about Corvina?"

Rion's eyes turned molten at the mention of the woman's name. The fire behind his eyes was blinding. His fingers curled into a tightly clenched fist before slamming it against the wood. "Do not utter her fucking name to me," he hissed.

"Why?" my uncle shot back. "Is your guilt eating away at your conscience? That girl *loved* you—she thought you hung the moon and stars for her and her alone."

Castor's pain was evident as his voice cracked, breaking my heart. I didn't know this woman or her connection to my family, but she was treasured. I knew that without a doubt.

Rion's eyes drifted close to stop his memories from running rampant. "Stop."

"How did you do it? I've searched, you know. Trying to find why every trace of her was erased from our memories and why you needed to hide it. The records of your union are sealed, redacted from public records as if that match was a mistake, but how did you make us —*her family*—forget she existed?"

I stopped breathing, unable to control my erratically beating heart as it began to fracture into jagged shards. *Redacted. Sealed.* I didn't want to think about the implications of my uncle's words because if his words were true...

"This is your last warning, Castor. Leave now, and we can forget this conversation took place."

"No," my uncle said, shaking his head. "I am not leaving here until you give me the answers I seek, nor will I be leaving without my niece. She doesn't deserve this."

"Is that so?" Rion said, leaning back in his chair. "And do you think Calia would go with you without explanation? Are you ready to give that to her?"

What was that supposed to mean?

"You are one to talk. What answers have you given when she's asked?" When Rion didn't answer, my uncle continued. "I will give her the truth as long as it gets her away from you and your family," he spat. "I will tell her every little fucking thing, every dirty secret, if that is what it takes. Do not test me, D'Arcy."

Rion growled. "And do not threaten *me*, Darrow. I allowed you into our home as a courtesy to my wife, but do not mistake that as free rein to insult me or my family. You have outstayed your welcome."

My uncle scoffed, crossing his arms. "The lies slip off your tongue better than any devil I met. You act as though you love her—"

"I do," Rion said without hesitation. "Not that I owe any explanation to you."

If I thought I couldn't breathe before, it paled in comparison to how I felt now. Rion showed his love through his actions, but neither of us had uttered the words out loud that would encase our bond in stone. But hearing them now after they'd been tainted by omissions made me sick.

It wasn't possible to love someone without giving them your all. And if you didn't bare your soul fully, then it couldn't possibly be love. I'd romanticized the emotion to a point where it had seemed unobtainable. Even now, the secrets Rion had been keeping close to his chest would always have me second-guessing if he was telling me the entire truth.

"I want to believe you, Rion, because Calia deserves every bit of happiness this life can offer, but if you loved her—*truly loved her*—you would have told her the truth by now."

The sound of fingertips drumming against hollow wood filled the silence before Rion spoke. "How am I supposed to explain my past without divulging my worst deeds, those actions which would taint me in her eyes? Am I not allowed to feel my regret privately?"

"Because not doing so is putting her in danger. I do

not have to impress upon you the consequences your silence will have—you know them already. The Vail is breathing down my back. There is only so much longer I can hold them off."

"And Calia? Do you think she can forgive me when she finds out?"

Castor sighed. "I believe she is more understanding than she should be, but this is beyond anything I can predict. Your story is unprecedented; there has never been a single person touched by the curse more than once. She will find out, D'Arcy. Whether you tell her or not."

"And you would be the one to do it?" Rion asked in warning. The thick, corded muscle in his neck thrummed along his pulse.

"If I need to be, then yes."

Rion bellowed in pain, his hands raking across the desk and sending the contents careening onto the floor. His chair fell back as he ran his fingers through his mussed hair. My uncle watched as the man I loved tore apart his study just as he had torn apart my heart.

"I will kill you if you tell her," he said, turning on my uncle with a vile gaze that turned my stomach.

"I should have forced your hand or killed you many moons ago, but here we are," Castor said, spreading his arms wide. "Standing in a mess of your family's making. You killed Corvina, Rion. Whether by accident or not, that scar etched upon your chest is a glaring reminder of how much she wanted to *live*."

"*Who hurt you?*" I'd asked him that question time

and time again, only to be met with a placating response that gave nothing away. Gods, I was so fucking stupid—a fool falling into bed with a man I barely knew .

I was too lost to hear the footsteps rounding the corner before it was too late. Strong hands gripped me from behind, pushed open the door, and threw me to the ground in front of the two men I'd loved more than anything. My head swam with their confessions, and I could no longer differentiate between reality and falsehood.

"Calia," Rion breathed, taking a step forward. He stopped when he saw the mascara-stained tear tracks running down my face. Only one thought formed in my mind, and I let him hear it.

I don't trust you. Stay away. Don't come closer.

Renwick and Leonora strode into the room, the former winding his thick fingers in my hair and jerking it upright. I couldn't stifle my scream as he pulled the strands taut and forced me to stare into Rion's silver gaze.

"Take your hands off her," he snarled. His staccato breaths and tight shoulders gave away his fear, but I didn't know if it was for my well-being or because he knew I'd heard everything.

"It is so nice to see you, Castor," Leonora purred. "Now, I do not have to leave my house to slit your throat."

"Perhaps your threat would hold some weight if I didn't already know you are absolute shit with a blade."

Her eyes narrowed into tiny slits before she turned

toward Rion. He clenched the side of his desk, the wood groaning underneath the white-knuckled pressure. "You've done well, son," Leonora said, walking over and patting him on the cheek. "She loves you more than she wants to admit—more than her sister ever did. Look at that hatred burning inside her."

"*Sister*?" I whispered, flicking my gaze between Castor and Rion. To my uncle's credit, at least he looked ashamed, but my husband's gaze was growing colder with every second.

"Yes," Renwick said, resting his lips along the shell of my ear. I tried to pull away, but his grip tightened once more until I cried out. "It's a shame, really. She was such a pretty little thing, so vibrant and full of life until Rion bled her dry."

I couldn't think, couldn't move—not as I stared back at the man I thought I knew. His words hit me like a bullet as I remembered what he said about his past love.

"*She was murdered.*" That's all he'd shared. I hadn't thought twice about the significance before, but now I felt sick. That fucking bastard. He had every opportunity to tell me the truth, yet he spat in my face with his omissions.

But I had no sister. My mother and father struggled to conceive me, and given how hard the birth was, they settled for me alone. Or so I thought.

"Look at me, baby. Please," Rion whispered, imploring me to obey just this once. "Please, just look at me…"

But I couldn't focus as my mind clouded, drowning me with wave after wave of confusion.

Leonora laughed, flitting her gaze between Rion and I. "Your family has kept so much from you, Calia, but you mustn't blame them. It was not their fault they had forgotten all about your poor sister." She ran her finger along Rion's shoulder as she spoke. "There isn't much money can't buy, and when you have pockets that run as deep as ours, you will find an answer for nearly every problem. Corvina Darrow and her *untimely* death were one of the biggest problems we have ever encountered, but even still, we found a way to make her disappear."

"What did you do to her?" I asked, attempting to steady my voice.

"The D'Arcy's have searched for a cure since the day this curse was placed on our people," Leonora began. "Time and time again, we were told nothing could be done. The magic used to bind us to our celestial bodies had vanished, taking the power to revert us back to our old selves with it. But twenty-five years ago, Rion's father stumbled upon a document taken from the old fae palace before it was burned to ash."

"Let me guess," I said sarcastically. "It said you needed Darrow blood."

Renwick tightened his grip at my remark, but Leonora nodded. "That has always been known, dear, but how the Darrow blood needed to be taken was the issue." She waited for understanding to dawn, smiling when she saw it in my eyes.

Love. It had to be given through love.

thirty-two

"You fucking bastard," I seethed, tempering my splintering heart in the process. Rion's pleading eyes fixed on me, imploring me to stop making snap judgments before he could explain himself. But our clock had run out, and we were now living on stolen time.

"Calia, please," he began again. His body visibly shook from the force needed to keep his emotions at bay, but it did nothing but stir my anger further.

"It was all a lie, wasn't it?" I thought as I sifted through our short-lived toxic history until realization dawned. "Oh, gods... That's why you've been trying to soften me up since the day of the attack, right? Because you knew after how you acted, I would never open that window of opportunity for you to climb through again."

I felt stupid, unimaginably so, and it was all my fault. Because I fell for a man who wanted to watch me bleed as he and his family prospered. "You *used* me, you *manipulated* me, and for what? So you can break a curse set in motion by both our ancestors?"

I felt the fracture of Rion's emotional state as he looked at me with a tear-filled gaze. "Listen to me, love. Please, let me ex—"

Renwick's ever-tightening grip sent new waves of pain as he clawed at my scalp before jerking my head to stare into soulless eyes. "Do you know how difficult it is to never walk amongst the majority, to sit by—wasting your life sitting in a house behind an enchanted barrier which does nothing but show us what we are missing? You should be thanking us for fighting so hard," he snarled, spittle flying out and splattering my face.

Rion lunged forward, barely avoiding me, to tackle Renwick. With a thud, I landed on the ground, scrambling toward my uncle, who grasped me in his arms. Something sharp dug into my thigh as I remembered the dagger Rowena had given me.

While Leonora was preoccupied watching Rion and Renwick struggle against each other, I slowly retrieved my blade and slid it into my uncle's waiting palm. He was far better with a weapon than I was, centuries of training honing him into the warrior he grew to be. He could end this, should I fail.

Not that it mattered because I knew only I could end this struggle. Only I could truly punish my husband for his deception.

The plan was there, forming in the back of my mind, but the strength I needed to execute it waned. If I went through with this, the wrath of those I loved would haunt me eternally.

It was a price I'd gladly pay, though, to ensure their safety.

"Enough!" Leonora shrieked, stomping over and grabbing each man by the neck. Long talons dug into their skin, drawing blood that ran in thick rivulets. Rion's chest rose and fell with heaving breaths, his eyes frantically scanning to see if I was safe.

I hated myself for how my heart faltered, because I would've moved mountains to ensure he never felt an ounce of pain again, even though he was ultimately responsible for the gaping wound in my chest. Even more so when his eyes softened with the knowledge I was unharmed.

But his relief would be short-lived, much like my elation had been to finally know what it felt like to be loved. Or so I thought.

Because if this was love, I didn't want it. How could someone claim that kind of dominion over another person yet lure them out under false pretenses? He demolished the wall I'd once built high, knocking it over with a wrecking ball of lies and half-truths. Ultimately, all I was left with was rubble, the broken pieces of our relationship.

I fought the nausea rising, standing on trembling legs. My uncle looked down, furrowing his brows in question. *What are you doing?* He seemed to say.

Shaking my head, I fought back tears, hoping it conveyed my message to him. *Trust me.*

I glanced toward the large window, captivated by the beauty of the stars against the inky sky. Even the blood moon was stunning, casting the world in a soft crimson glow. But that attraction was stolen by what it represented—the horrors that would be unleashed on this night.

"Now, girl," Leonora said, striding past both men until she stood before me. "It is time to give us what we seek. Do it willingly, and you may leave. No one will stop you." She pulled a long black dagger from behind her back, the edge glinting with the promise of imminent death.

No matter what words she used, we all knew she'd never allow me to leave. Not alive, anyway.

Her tongue flicked out and danced across the tip of her lengthening fangs as her eyes devoured me as if I were the answer to every prayer she'd ever uttered. Which, I supposed, wasn't far off from the truth.

"How does the blood need to be given?" I asked, wiping my sweat-coated palms across the back of my dress.

"Mother, no," Rion growled, attempting to stand, but Renwick forced him down. There was so much distance between us, even in such a small space. He felt it. I could see that from the frantic look in his eyes as he clawed at his uncle's grip as he glanced between Leonora and I. "No, I will not let you do this."

I leveled him with a blank stare, unable to muster any malice or misery. "You no longer have a say in my decisions."

"Calia, listen she—"

"How does the blood need to be given?" I asked again, ignoring Rion entirely. I couldn't stand watching him fight to get to me, or how hearing his pleading words made me want to believe the sincerity interwoven into each syllable. If I focused too long, I wouldn't go through with this.

Leonora walked toward an unassuming painting on the wall, pulling it off to reveal a safe. She brought her thumb to her teeth, using the sharp edge to coax blood to the surface. "There are two ways," she began, placing her finger on the lock. The turning of multiple gears filled the room, and I waited on bated breath for her to drop the truth I knew was coming.

"The first, I would say, is the 'traditional' way—a true joining between vampyre and fae. You would each take from one another until you were nearly spent, ingesting the other's essence, power, and memories. It relies on trust. You must trust one another to ensure neither goes past the point of no return."

"You mean death."

She dipped her head once in confirmation. "The second is more formal, but just as effective." She reached inside and produced a silver chalice, the outside lined with a mixture of onyx and ruby jewels. "It is an offering, a mixture of your blood with Rion's until the chalice is filled. Then it is to be blessed by a descendant of the sorceress who placed the curse upon our families under the light of the red moon."

I blinked in surprise. "I was under the impression

there was none. If they'd been around all along, why has it been so difficult to break the—"

"Enough questions. Give me your arm, girl."

I cradled my arm to my chest, needing to buy more time. "If I'm giving my blood to your cause, I deserve to have answers."

"You are not going to be giving anything," Rion spat, finally breaking free of Renwick's hold. He sped to my side, grabbing my face and forcing me to look at him.

"Do not touch her," my uncle snarled, but his protests fell on unsympathetic ears.

I struggled against Rion's hold, clawing at his skin until I felt wetness underneath my nails. "Let me go," I said through gritted teeth. All the color leached away from his eyes, their manic silver glow nearly blinding as he stared me down. His hold on me grew unbearably tight, my panic apparent as tears began to fall. "Dammit, let me go." My quivering voice was barely audible as I started beating on his chest.

"You are hurting her!" my uncle shouted, leaping for me. Renwick surged forward, catching him by the throat and slamming him against the wall. My view was obstructed, but I heard the swift motion of a blade cutting through flesh.

No, no, no! The chant echoed in my mind, screaming at me to go to my uncle and ensure his safety. Still, I couldn't do anything but stare into my husband's terrified gaze. It wasn't until I heard Leonora's shriek of anger that I allowed a modicum of relief to reach my panic-stricken heart.

Rion loosened his grip momentarily, but it was enough to allow me to watch Renwick fall to his knees, grasping at his neck. My uncle stood over his flailing body, glancing between Renwick and the dagger in his hands. Smoke rose from the blade, the stench of burning flesh filling the air.

In anger, Leonora flew toward Rion and me, breaking his hold. I pulled away, gasping for air as she turned on me with a vicious glint in her darkening eyes. "What magic is this?" she seethed, turning back to watch Renwick grow deathly still, his pallor grey and mottled. Her gaze dipped to the empty sheath attached to my thigh. "Who gave you that blade?"

I opened my mouth, unable to admit it was her own daughter who'd given me the knife. There'd been no distinction, no warning or words spoken which would have clued me in to the power it possessed.

As she lunged toward me, Rion stepped in her path and obscured me from her view. "Do not fucking touch her." His voice boomed, rattling the glass of the windows. Small cracks began forming, reaching for one another in desperation which mirrored my own. "She is mine."

Castor met my gaze over Rion's shoulder, time slowing to an unbearable crawl. He saw my resolve, realization turning to horror as I stepped back until I felt the paned glass of the window. Rion and Leonora were locked in a stalemate, vibrating with the force of their anger as the other stood in the way of what they wanted.

"I am no one's," I said, forcing my voice to remain

even as all eyes turned toward me. Rion's glowing gaze simmered with rage, his fists clenched at his sides.

"Calia," my uncle warned, taking a step toward me, but I shook my head for him to stay.

I could give him a distraction, time to escape, and tell the council what Leonora's plans were. But there was only one way for me to do so. For him, for my family, and for the future of our world, I had to be strong.

I wanted to heed the call of the moon just as much as they wanted to feel the warmth of the sun. Still, something about Leonora and Renwick's simple explanation didn't make sense. Why had they searched for so long yet still been unable to free themselves?

Breathe, Calia. Breathe.

"What are you doing, girl?" Leonora growled.

I looked at Rion, forcing a smile that cleaved my soul. "It was always going to end like this. One way or another." Rion stepped forward as I pushed open the window and felt the chill of the evening air on my skin. It wouldn't take long to feel the sting of the moon's violent crimson light.

He shook his head, those silver eyes clearing briefly before they widened in terror. "Calia... Love..." he rasped, but it was too late. My decision had already been made.

This was my reality. I was a sacrificial offering in every sense of the word. My life had been destined to be intertwined with his from the moment I was born. I'd never had a chance to come into my own, but my choices now would change that. For once, the power would lie in my hands. No matter how it ended, I would be responsible for forging my path.

I took a deep breath, summoning my strength as all three watched with apprehension. Rion and Leonora could make it to me in a second, stopping me if they desired. Rion lifted his foot, preparing to move as he understood my plan.

With one last look, I reached back, my palm colliding with the cracked glass of the windowpane, unfeeling even as the shards tore into my flesh. With one last look, I stepped out into the vermillion dark. The distant echo of screams reached me, tears falling down my cheeks as the faded glow of the blood moon shined down on my descent.

rion

I stared out at the horizon, searching for a thready pulse in a symphony of solid beats as the bleary darkness of another night faded into the muted glow of a pointless day. The events of last night still lingered in the air, a phantom guilt I thought I'd shed when Calia had arrived. Lifting the bottle of liquor to my lips, the sharp tang of whiskey burned as it slid down my throat.

I welcomed the pain. I imagined each pull was a mouthful of jagged glass, intended to rip muscle and flesh until I drowned in my own blood. Even that would have been less painful than the truth. Oh, the irony—given that the truth had played a part in her demise.

I closed my eyes against the onslaught of images unrelentlessly flitting from one to the other without reprieve. From the moment I saw her, intrinsically knowing she was mine in every sense of the word, to our panic-addled end which had assured my ruination.

I don't trust you.

Stay away.

Don't come closer.

I am no one's.

I had not lied when I said I could pick out her thoughts in a room of thousands. It was why I knew she was crouching outside the door of my office last night, before it all went to shit. Somehow, I assumed letting her see my warring indecision might have softened the blow of my omissions.

The admission of my feelings came too late—something a better man would have known. But I was *not* a better man; I was the devil who haunted her dreams, turning them into nightmares.

Had she given in to my mother's demands, Calia would have died by her hand. My mother was never going to let her live. She had dedicated her life to the curse, and she would do whatever it took to ensure Calia was the final obstacle in her way. I had heard them, Leonora's plans to rip into Calia's throat, Renwick's plot to hold me in compulsion as my mother bled her into my open mouth. Calia hadn't seen the smirk that crossed my mother's face as I shouted for her to stop.

I brought the bottle up again, downing the remaining amber liquid trapped inside. Nearly gagging as the thought of Calia's blood filled my mind. The door behind me opened, soft footsteps padding against the wooden floor. I turned without looking, throwing the now useless vessel across the room. It landed against the wall, shattering with a deafening crash next to Jasper's feet.

"What?" I barked, turning toward the window to watch the rest of the world come alive. Mortals and supernaturals peppered the landscape—living their mundane lives and laughing while my world imploded. I had no way of knowing who they were, but I hated every single one of them. They did not know the fear coursing through my veins or understand the depth of my rage.

For once, I had possessed what I had always wanted in the palm of my hand, and it had been ripped away, shredded, and left in tatters. The memory of her touch lingered on my skin, decimating my heart with guilt and longing.

"Rion," he began, stopping abruptly as my hand slammed against the window. The glass rattled and cracked underneath the force, and I wished it had shattered and left me burning. I knew why he was here, how the news he clutched in his white-knuckle grip would force me to confront another truth I did not want to face.

"Please," I whispered, closing my eyes to stifle the onslaught of grief threatening to break free.

Jasper set the crumpled letter down on the bar cart beside me, placing a heavy hand on my shoulder. Only then, with the realization that complete and utter silence had fallen, did I allow myself to fall to my knees and weep.

meet amber

Amber Palmer is an American fantasy romance author. She was born in Arizona, but raised in Texas. She is the proud parent of three (evil) cats and one puppy dog, and when she isn't nose deep in a spicy fantasy novel, she's listening to her bookish Spotify playlists and making notes for her next project! A passionate advocate for mental health, Amber features characters processing various traumas in her work. She is an unapologetic lover of anything spicy, while also making time to game with her husband.

facebook.com/amberpalmerauthor

instagram.com/amberpalmerauthor

amazon.com/Amber-Palmer/e/B09MN1M59K

tiktok.com/@amberpalmerauthor

goodreads.com/amber_palmer